The Prince Saga: Volume 1

S.Nasonov

S.Nasonov

Contents

.

To my husband who's constant tirade of ideas were more helpful than he could ever know.

To Molly, for unwavering hype up support.

1

"Excellent news, Mary!" A boisterous male voice echoed off the walls of the indoor playground. Mary looked up from the padded triangle she was wiping to see her boss' panting frame. His cheeks were ruddy and brow was damp with excitement.

Or perhaps he had taken the stairs? Good for him.

Mary liked Mr. Malinowski, he was kind and fair and paid her slightly above minimum wage. He had round glasses that matched his round physique. His upturned mustache wriggled as he spoke, reminding Mary of those hairy caterpillars she never allowed herself to touch.

"My sweet Esmeralda convinced her sister, you know the one who manages the library, to let us run an informational booth!" he finished exuberantly. Mary did not personally know Esmeralda or her library managing sister, but felt like it was not appropriate to mention it at that moment. Mr. M frequently prattled on about one problem or another, and Mary was always happy to listen.

Mary rested the damp silver-impregnated

rag on the padded mat. The texture of the microfiber cloth made her palms itch– if Mary was in charge she would outlaw microfiber outright, but she was not the boss here. The actual boss was looking at her with excited expectation.

Had he said something she was supposed to respond to?

Mr. M did not hire her for stellar intellect or exceptional skill– Mary was well aware her main positive attribute was unconditional tolerance. She was completely unphased by emotional outbursts or temper tantrums– a useful trait when one was forced to interact with toddlers and their parents. Although her role was only to sanitize play equipment and set up for birthday parties, she often found herself being a confidant to those around her.

This job had taught Mary many things, some more useful than others. She was exceptionally good at spotting hand foot and mouth disease on sticky toddler fingers, and could unwrap a cheese string in less than five seconds. Some may see those skills as insignificant, but Mary was optimistic by nature. She was also prone to a wandering mind.

Mr. M cleared his throat, waiting for Mary to inquire further about his latest venture.

"An informational booth." Mary repeated.

Was there another measles outbreak? That kid yesterday looked a bit rashy. Mary should have said something– she took the safety of the other children very seriously. The indoor play area was situated in a rather affluent neighborhood, the vaccination rates were likely too low for herd immunity. It made Mary snort that rich people thought they were impervious to infectious diseases.

Rich people made Mary the most nervous—she was always worried she would say something to offend them.

"Precisely." Mr. M confirmed, finger lifting in the air.

Mary hummed and nodded, attempting to sound interested. Truthfully she didn't care about whatever the portly man was scheming, but she had a feeling it directly implicated her.

"The topic is relevant, prudent, and most

importantly, life saving." The man gesticu-
lated wildly with his puffy hands, a sheen of
excitement on his face.

Mary wasn't keen to believe him, considering he thought silver weaved rags were ade-
quately antibacterial.

Mary nodded and continued to wipe, picturing the armies of tiny microbes dueling on a
battlefield of microfiber.

"Well, don't you want to know the details?"
Mr. M asked, tone now tinged with impatience. Mary sat up instantly and placed the
rag and spray bottle on her lap, demonstrat-
ing rapt attention.

"Yes, of course. Please tell me." she smiled
and nodded politely. Mary kicked herself internally for making him feel like she wasn't

interested.

Well, she wasn't interested but he didn't need to know that.

"Carbon monoxide poisoning!" he exploded, flaying his hands out in what she would consider jazz hands.

Mary's mouth popped open in surprise. Mr. M took this as an invitation to keep speaking.

"After we lost our darling Ronald last September I fell into despair. Cheryl, you know with large hair and small lips-" he began again. Mary recalled that was his grief counselor. "She said action may be a more constructive way to process my grief as opposed to weeping incessantly." he finished, his brown eyes were strong and earnest.

Mary recalled that Ronald was Mr. M's elderly Pomeranian. They found him unresponsive in the garage a few months prior, with no official cause of death. (He did not want to 'disgrace Ronald's resting spirit' by having a necropsy done.)

Mr. M subsequently became obsessed with the possibility that a carbon monoxide leak was the cause, after seeing a PSA during the commercial break of his soap opera. When he was rambling about it Mary couldn't help imagining Ronald attaching a dog sized hose to a dog sized tail pipe.

Perhaps he'd had a mental breakdown from being separated from his food dish.

Mary suspected obesity was the likely culprit of his sudden demise, as Ronald looked more like a sausage with legs than a dog. Nevertheless, clearly this was important to Mr. Malinowski, and Mary was obligated to help.

"I didn't know you moonlight as a safety educator." she clarified, surprised he'd never mentioned it before. The man shared most of his thoughts, feelings, and bodily functions. Mary stood, tucking the bottle and rag into her arm pit.

"I don't," he said gripping her shoulders warmly, "but I do know a beautiful, smart, and obedient young employee who would be willing to share this important and life saving information." she felt his grip intensify when he spoke of her obedience, as if needing to remind her.

She shook off his hold gently. Mary was short and stout with plain features –clearly, Mr. M was trying to use flattery to grease her into agreeing. Mary didn't usually require much coercion, she made it a point of pride to be helpful. She was, however, petrified at the idea of being so exposed.

"I'm not sure I would do a great job. I don't know anything about carbon monoxide or its hazards." she said tentatively, walking over to the storage closet and placing the cleaning supplies on the shelf. Mr. M wad- dled behind her, close on her heels.

"Yes, but even if one life is saved my heart can rebuild." he held his chest emphatically. "Besides, it'll all be in the pamphlet. All you have to do is stand there and look approachable." he instructed.

Easier said than done.

Mary didn't consider herself particularly approachable, her mother always chastised her for scrunching her eyebrows together when she wasn't paying attention. She tried to put on a charismatic front, especially when she was tasked with doing things she wasn't interested in. She found herself using empathy to rationalize a particularly dull request.

Mary suspected that sweet Esmeralda had something to do with this bizarre idea. Last week Mr. M mentioned his wife had to put an ointment on his face twice a day for 'tear-related dermatitis'.

Mary could imagine that caring for the dramatic man would be laborious and exhausting. It seemed like a very reasonable trade– Mary's lone suffering in exchange for the survival of Mr. M's whole family. She had to do this; if she didn't he could fly off the handle, get a messy and expensive divorce, be forced to sell his business, and she would be left unemployed.

Mary could do this. For Esmeralda.

"Alright." she agreed, giving him the warmest smile she could muster.

2

M r. Malinowski clearly overestimated the interest of the general public for carbon monoxide safety awareness.

She was only one hour into her booth duty and it was looking grim. Mary did her best– the smile she plastered on her face was large if not a little forced. She made a solid attempt to find answers to questions she was wildly unprepared for, to not fail miserably and disappointed her boss.

"Does it smell that bad?" a teenage boy asked, his frame was made up of mostly curly hair and hoodie. Mary could still see the look of disgust on his face.

"Oh, um, it's odorless actually, it just occupies the place in your lungs where oxygen should be." Mary had done a small amount of research the night before, so she was confident on the basics. In high school Mary had discovered that her performance anxiety had a very simple exploit: purpose. If she had a job to do, the spotlight didn't threaten to burn her alive. They wouldn't be judging her as a person, only the information she was communicating. It was an important mind trick that made the panic of being seen recede.

Most of the time.

She placed her shaking palms behind her, hoping the boy couldn't smell her fear.

He scoffed and walked off, allowing Mary to release the breath she was holding.

Although her nerves were fried, Mary was grateful someone talked to her at all— a small group of tween girls just pointed and laughed when she was setting up the display.

Hours passed and her stack of pamphlets remained untouched. Disappointment began to build in Mary's chest –not one person had scanned the QR code on her shirt. Fortunately, she did run out of stickers after the first

Mommy-and-me story time class, but she was skeptical that toddlers were the target population to begin with.

Mary thought it was bizarre to have a reading class for babies since she was almost certain they couldn't read.

"Um, excuse me, miss. Your fart cloud is falling down." a gentle male voice spoke.

Mary looked up to see a young, well dressed man pointing towards the top portion of her booth. She stuck her head out and partially climbed onto the plastic surface, trying to understand what the man was talking about.

The green plywood cloud cut out that was hanging above her really did resemble a cartoon fart. It certainly didn't help that the banner had 'Silent and Deadly' in large bubble letters. The graphic was listing dramatically to one side, hanging on for dear life. Mary suddenly felt the need to hold on to something as well, flooding horror making her head spin. Mary assumed it was meant to represent carbon monoxide gas, which was both factually incorrect and artistically bankrupt.

Mary threw her head back and groaned. No wonder nobody was seriously interested in her message— It appeared she was educating on the dangers of errant flatulence. Her misery was interrupted when the slippery pamphlets beneath her palm shifted and tumbled towards the gray carpet. Mary should have been concerned about the fact this caused her side to slam down painfully on the booth table, but the only thing that wounded her was the loud sound and paper mess she made with her clumsiness.

"Oh, god. Are you okay?" the man asked, reaching his hand out to help her up.

He was an acceptable height for a man, definitely under six feet but not by much. He could have been taller but there was a significant hunch to his posture, like he wasn't comfortable taking up space. It made her sad for him, he was quite slim so she couldn't imagine he took up much space.

Following Archimedes' principle, he wouldn't displace many of the molecules around him. If he was in the bath the water would doubtfully rise more than a few inches. His long spindly legs would probably hang out of Mary's small tub, though. She was grateful she had a tub at all, considering how little rent she paid. Her apartment was a run down little studio– working part time at a children's playground did not afford her a luxurious life. No, this man would likely need to have a shower if he came over.

Mary shook her head to clear the image of this stranger bathing in her apartment.

His long fingers were cool against hers as she swiveled herself to a seated position, legs hanging over the front edge of the booth. A warm tingle remained when he let go of her hand, a stark contrast to the comforting cadence of his voice. Face flushing with embarrassment, Mary trained her gaze down towards the pile of pamphlets on the ground.

They lay discarded and disgraced, closely mirroring her professional integrity.

"I got it." the man said before she could hop down to grab them. He dropped to his knees, collecting the sheets of glossy paper and handing them to her in a neat stack. Mary's breath stalled when he looked up at her.

He looked like a prince.

He was not classically handsome, his face was largely overpowered by a nose which was decorated with a noticeable bump in the center. Mary wondered whether it was a natural deformity or if he had broken it in the past.

Would that make him sexier?

Mary's mother would frequently make vulgar remarks about the stars of action films, especially when they were half naked and covered in the blood of their enemies. Mary never really understood the appeal, but to each their own. She preferred men that could hold a decent conversation more than anything. This man certainly didn't look like he was brimming with uncontrolled testosterone. He was pale, with a smattering of purple under his eyes. His hair was nicely done, only a few locks escaping to dangle in front of his eyes. Those eyes were blue and deep. Mary felt an unexplained pull to keep looking into those eyes. To tell him all of her secrets.

No, he was not especially beautiful.

To her, he was perfect.

"Oh, um, thank you." she finally spoke, her higher brain function returning. A flash of fear filled the blue globes and his gaze was gone, breaking the mesmerizing connection. He nodded, grabbed a pamphlet, and walked away.

Mary watched the mysterious man as he walked and sat at one of the tables at the back, squarely between the mystery and fantasy sections.

He was a mysterious fantasy indeed.

His movements were awkward and lethargic as he pulled out a novel from his bag. His fatigue and business attire led Mary to believe he had come from work.

Mary's chest tingled; she always appreciated a man that was employed. Guilt followed
quickly after– the man had exhausted himself at work all day and she let him pick up
her mess.

The rest of Mary's shift was uneventful,
mostly due to the fact that her focus was on
the sickly man at the back of the room.

Her work schedule returned to usual, early mornings three times a week. Mary found her thoughts lingering on the lonesome stranger as she wiped a suspiciously urine-coloured puddle from underneath the miniature trampoline.

Did he come to the library regularly?

What did he do there?

Mary had many challenges –impulse control was one of them.

This fascination was completely out of character for her. Mary was a good level-headed girl. She went to work everyday and did her job to her best ability. She did not become infatuated with the first stranger that got down on his knees for her.

Did he actually get on his knees for her?

Technically he knelt down to clean up her mess, which was just as novel. Mary wasn't used to having anyone clean up her messes. It was usually the other way around, as evidenced by the suspicious brown smudge that was left on the disturbing microfiber cloth. There was no way that man would ever actually get down on his knees for her, not in the way her deviant mind suddenly materialized.

The image of her new obsession kneeling for her on purpose was too salacious to be believed.

Besides, if he was interested he would have talked to her. Men were not shy in their advances, from her experience. However, the concept of a submissive man was not completely foreign to her – one of her previous boyfriends had enjoyed being pegged. It didn't particularly arouse Mary but she was a pretty tolerant person and had a hard time rejecting people.

One time she jokingly asked a man to beg and he laughed just at the suggestion. That rejection felt like a very large and hot knife in her chest. Mary would rather swallow an entire clutch of spider eggs than make anyone feel that way.

Mary was comfortable with her role as the happy recipient of romantic intentions. It was easy and simple. Nobody got hurt that way, especially not her.

So why couldn't she get the idea of that helpful man worshiping her out of her mind?

"Mary, darling." Mr. M crept up behind her, almost startling the apple sauce pouch right out of her hand. "How did it go?" he inquired, hands clutching the lapels of his crushed velvet blazer.

Mary swallowed. She didn't want to upset him with the truth of her failure—she'd prefer to stop thinking about it altogether.

"There were some technical difficulties, but we really cracked the infant demographic I think." Mary shut the fridge door and turned to face her boss. Instead of gratitude his mustached face sported disappointment.

A painful cramp gripped Mary's stomach.

One of Mary's other flaws was inability to

take criticism. Well, she could take it but she would be crying about it in the supply closet later.

"About that..." Mr. M began, lips pressed together in pity. Mary steeled herself, ready for the termination of her employment.

"I'm sorry." Mary apologized, unable to stop herself. Perhaps she could salvage the situation with enough begging and logical explanation. "The fart cloud was falling down, and I slipped on the pamphlets. The paper was of a very high quality, too glossy in fact. It was bad. No, I mean I was bad-" she spiraled, breaths fast and shallow.

"Mary," Mr. M grabbed Mary by the shoulders and shook vigorously. "Snap out of it."

Mary took a deep breath when the shaking

had stopped.

"Sorry, please continue." she said politely, head still swimming.

"This is precisely what I wanted to speak to you about." Mr. M began, turning and sashaying towards the break room. Mary followed behind him, heart hammering in time with his speedy gallop.

"I'll be the first to admit that I haven't been the best employer." he said, pulling out a rusted foldable chair for Mary before sitting on his own.

"No, don't say that-" she began but Mr. M held up his hand to stop her.

"I've been working you too hard. Look at you, you're a nervous wreck." he gestured towards her. Truthfully, Mary hadn't been nervous at all until he started this conversation. The older man sighed, a sympathetic look in his eyes.

"You're going on vacation."

Mary blinked.

"No I'm not?" her words sounded more like a question, despite the fact that she was very certain she had no trip planned. Mary had never been on a vacation as an adult. Her father had taken her to DisneyLand as a child, but he was so absorbed with his work phone she was basically alone. She did enjoy the churros, though.

Mr. M nodded somberly. "Yes, you are. I feel an obligation for your physical and mental health. You are going off for a week on compassionate leave." His eyes were wide and he scooped her hands into his big meaty paws.

"Compassionate leave? Who needs the compassion?" Mary couldn't hide the confusion from slipping onto her face. She didn't have any dying family members as far as she could remember.

"You," he said, "from me." he placed a gentle kiss on the back of her hand. Mary withdrew her hands from his weirdly affectionate grip. She wasn't sure what was going on with her boss, but decided she probably didn't want to know.

"It may be unpaid, but I am sure the rest will be revitalizing." he reassured, standing abruptly and turning to leave the pathetic excuse for a break room. "Besides, it's important to do something nice for yourself."

3

Mary visited the library every day of her forced vacation. She told herself it was the most economically sound decision, but in reality she was hoping to see her handsome stranger again.

She puttered around her miniscule apartment for the entire morning before she found herself getting on the bus. She had washed, dried, and folded every article of clothing she owned, vacuumed, mopped, and dusted every available surface and still had several hours left before lunch. The entire time she worked her bosses' words rang in her ear.

"Do something nice for yourself." she grumbled, aggressively scrubbing the grout of her kitchen floor.

Her mother always said the nicest thing anyone could do for themselves was to get their life together.

Mary's life was together enough, wasn't it?

So what if she had no love, friendship, money, status, or power?

She had integrity and discipline, and that was more important in self-indulgence. Selfish people were hurtful, and that was the opposite of what she wanted. When her back was too sore to continue, Mary took a break.

She had made an attempt to read, but found her mind wandering off of the ink on the page and back to the mysterious stranger from the library.

Perhaps she just needed a more interesting book, something so salacious it would distract her mind from edging towards obsession.

Yes, that was a very good honorable reason to visit the library. It had nothing to do with the bolt of excitement that ran through her at the thought of seeing him again.

The ache of disappointment lingered in her

chest as she browsed the shelves leisurely. Of course he wouldn't be there during the day, most people worked during business hours.

Unless he worked a sexy night time job. That would explain how exhausted he looked.

Mary bit her lip as she considered what deviant professions her muse could have.

Mary shook her head– he looked more like a night auditor than a stripper or escort. Her breath hitched when she imagined leaning over the counter of a fancy hotel and pulling him closer by the tie around his neck. His blue eyes would flash with fear, followed by hungry arousal.

Would he be too shy to throw her down on the counter and ravage her?

It was hard to fantasize about a man she knew nothing about. Some women could insert their crush into a daydream of their wishing, but Mary didn't feel right even imagining the man do something he didn't want to do. She took consent very seriously, and there was nothing sexier than yearning.

No, she couldn't truly fantasize about him until she got a better sense of his character.

As if called by her naughty thoughts, the mystery man walked through the automatic glass doors and towards the table at the back. Mary quickly hid behind a row of books, watching him through a small slit between the covers.

Looking at him in secret felt sensual, voyeuristic. He was on display for her while she was hidden, safe from his gaze. No one would know about her lapse in morality.

He wore the same white button down, dress pants and brown leather shoes as the day before. He still looked like he didn't quite eat enough or get enough sleep. Mary had the sudden and uncontrollable urge to feed him and tuck him into bed, and not in the fun sexy way. Well, maybe after.

Mary didn't know much, but she knew that staring at a stranger was creepy behavior. She couldn't go to the library just to stare at a possibly ill, unconventionally handsome man.

No, she needed to create plausible deniability of her deranged fascination.

Mary took the necessary precautions.

She continued to wear her "Say NO to CO!" shirt, to create an alibi for her likely future arrest.

No officer, this man simply looked so sickly he needed her close supervision.

Yes, she was an expert as per her shirt, and he was free to scan the QR code for more information.

Yes, she was aware that carbon monoxide is both colorless and odorless and her shirt was a personal insult to the field of chemistry.

To add to her alibi, Mary figured she should look like she was doing something normal and not stalker-like. Mary sat a reasonable distance away from him and began to scribble in a spare notebook she kept in her backpack, the princely stranger on her mind.

She allowed herself to glance at him after every paragraph, carefully not to arouse too much suspicion. Excitement throbbed inside her–this game fueled a fire in her loins that she never knew existed. Mary began to imagine that a man like that could look at her, could want her.

Who would she need to be in order to deserve complete devotion?

Mary's mind reeled with the delusion of arousal, longing to feel the heat of sexual power.

Mistress was sitting at the vanity, brushing the dull locks of hair when a soft knock at the door startled her. Her heart beat began to race just knowing he was near. She slowly crossed the plain room, floor boards creaking. The door knob shook in her grasp, the skin of her hands slick with anxiety.

The looks he gave her from his seat at the grand dining table burned in her memory. The burn of his fingers caressing her leg as she placed his meal in front of him, still lingered behind her knee.

"Good evening, miss. May I come in?" he said, mischief in his blue eyes. His lithe frame stood comfortably in the doorway, as if this too be-longed to him.

She took a deep breath. "I'm not sure that is ap-

propriate, your majesty." Her breath and words were shaky. "To be visiting a common girl's private quarters." she finished, stepping aside so he could enter the room.

He looked opulent surrounded by the blandness of the decor, the gold trim and satin finishes of his clothes stark against the worn wood. He was handsome and regal, a diamond amongst river stones.

"I don't know what common girl you speak of, I only see a goddess." His tone was casual but his gaze was heated. Before Mistress could react the Prince grabbed the back of her head and slammed their mouths together, pressing her up against the door.

Their tongues tangled deeply, bodies pressed close.

"My siren calls me with her full lips and plentiful curves." he began, voice strained with passion. "Beckons me closer with her coy smiles. I am lost to her." he moaned, peppering her neck and chest with kisses. His hands kneaded her rear underneath the cotton slip, causing the woman to arch her back. She clutched the back of the Prince's head, pulling his face into her aching breasts.

She could not let him win.

"I am no siren, but you are most definitely lost." she panted. "A Prince who is wandering, hoping for a release inside a girl of no notice." she finished, heat flooding her core at his ministrations. "A woman who could be discarded."

"No." he groaned and pulled away, a rush of air cooling her damp skin. "I am a man who is

desperate for you. What must I do to convince you of my intentions?" he demanded, his chest rising and falling hard. She could see the obvious tenting of his trousers, indicating his physical need for her. Mistress pondered his question for a moment.

How could the Prince show her she was more than a frivolous conquest?

"On your knees." she commanded.

A sudden throb between her legs caused Mary to pause writing. She did not expect to have such a physical reaction to the Prince's devotion. She glanced up at her muse who was reading peacefully, face concentrated as usual.

Would Mary like the real prince to kneel for her?

What if he saw her as the Prince saw his Mistress? An answering throb radiated into her womb.

The Prince dropped to his knees, blue eyes locked to his Mistress.

"If I order you to pleasure me with your mouth, will you obey? Will you still spend your time with me if I said you will not be getting your own release?" she asked, running her hands through his hair gently. He closed his eyes for a moment, relishing in her touch.

"It would be an honor, my goddess." he purred, turning his head to suckle on her arm. He haphazardly lifted her skirts and placed a leg over his shoulder, eagerly diving into her sex.

Mary shut her notebook forcefully, causing nearby patrons to glance her way including her prince. The skin of her cheeks heated, matching the unbearable scorch in her core. Heat pulsed in her veins at the thought of her prince's devotion.

She ran to the nearest bathroom, praising the deity above it was only a single stall. Mary was a needy beast in that moment, only aware of the pulsing between her legs. Thoughts of her prince on his knees flooded her mind.

How would his hair feel in her hands?

How skilled was his tongue?

What would his eyes look like as he worshiped her?

She shoved her hands into her panties, rubbing furiously until she reached a short but intense orgasm. Mary waited until her skin cooled and breaths slowed before washing her hands and collecting her thoughts.

She was a plain girl, unlikely to catch the eye of a man, let alone his submission. That sort of thing was only for tall, attractive, slender charismatic women in leather outfits.

Mary returned to her seat, mind and body calm once again. She didn't miss the smirk of the prince's face as she packed up her belongings.

She had a feeling it had nothing to do with the book he was reading.

4

Mary continued her perverted surveillance until one afternoon, when a disaster of unconscionable proportions occurred.

Her usual seat was taken.

All of the seats were taken.

Except for the one next to the princely stranger.

Of course.

She quickly hid behind a bookshelf and pondered her next move.

Maybe she should cut her losses and move to another continent. Certainly that would be more feasible than sitting next to her mysterious stranger.

Without looking up from his book, he pulled out the chair next to him.

"You can sit next to me, I won't bite." he said. His voice was a soft tenor, gentle and comforting.

Her loins clenched in response, but her legs remained frozen.

She had two viable choices at that moment: stay where she was now, or go and sit next to the man that had infiltrated her mind consistently since she'd first laid eyes on him. It seemed too self-indulgent, too easy to just sit next to the star of her fantasies.

Surely there could be a morally sound reason to talk to him?

Perhaps this was a sign from the universe that she could help him in some way.

It could be a subtle cry for help.

Mary's chest hummed at the possibility of aiding this man in any way, thawing out her immobile feet.

She cleared her throat and abandoned her hiding place, riding the high of panic to the plastic seat. Mary was not prepared for her prince to see her. She was suddenly very aware of the tightness of her pants, her posture, and her breath.

Did she smell? She figured she could go another day between showers but maybe not. This was precisely why Mary preferred to remain hidden.

"Thank you," she said politely, and pulled out her notebook as normal.

Mary was conscious of his eyes on her as she uncapped her pen. Was he looking at her out of curiosity or contempt?

Was he uncomfortable with her presence?

She had never seen him talk to anyone at this table before.

Should she excuse herself and give him some space?

She took in a deep breath to steady herself and simultaneously caught a whiff of her prince.

He smelled like deodorant and laundry detergent. Light and simple. Mary's heartbeat quieted at the scent, grounding her racing thoughts. He was just a man that was reading his book at the library and likely suffered from insomnia or a wasting disease. Maybe he just needed a friend. Mary couldn't do much, but she could be nice.

She smiled to herself and turned to him.

"How did you know I needed to sit?" she asked. His eyes shifted up to hers widening slightly, as if he did not expect there to be more conversation.

"Ah, my carbon monoxide detector went off." He said, eying the cloud on her shirt. Embarrassment flashed through her, she suddenly felt the need to strip that shirt off and burn it.

"I-" she started.

"I'm joking," he interrupted, a small smile dancing on his lips. "I saw that your usual seat was taken." he confessed, her chest burned at his words. She was shocked that he noticed where she usually sat, Mary wasn't used to being noticed. In fact, she usually preferred to be the one noticing others.

A long stretch of silence sat between them. They did not speak, but the hum of background whispers was soothing.

She observed him out of the corner of her eye, careful not to make her ogling too no-ticeable. From this distance she could see that the dark hair that flopped in front of his eyes was streaked with silver.

Perhaps her prince was older than she had originally thought.

She was still assessing him for crows feet when he spoke again.

"I like your shirt." he said, glancing down to the toxic green cloud graphic again. His eyes were more relaxed this time, as if he had permission to speak.

"Thank you. I, too, like to wear the same clothes repeatedly." Mary replied, and immediately regretted it. "I mean, I'm sure you have multiple shirts that you alternate and not just wear the same dirty shirt every-day, because that would make you smell and you do not smell." she blurted out with the speed, intensity, and finesse of a fatal motor vehicle accident.

She kicked herself internally. That was a creepy thing to say. He was going to call the police and she was going to spend the rest of her life whittling a ball point pen into a shiv and playing the harmonica.

Thoroughly embarrassed, Mary stood up. "Right then, I'm just gonna go-" she mumbled.

He grabbed her arm, halting her escape attempt. His skin was cool and slightly damp, but his fingers were so long that they wrapped fully around her forearm. Mary was impressed, her hands couldn't even wrap around her wrist. Mary wasn't sure if that would be due to having large forearm circumference or abnormally small hands. His hands were definitely much larger than hers. Intrusive thoughts of testing the size of his hand on her breast heated her core and hardened her nipples.

"No." he insisted, his eyes wide with pan-ic. "Stay." At that moment he wanted her to stay next to him, and she had the power to walk out the door.

Would he be disappointed?

Would he continue to think about her after she left?

Would he be happy if she stayed? Would he smile again? Mary had an undeniable need to make him smile again.

"Okay." she said, smiling softly. Her words snapped him back to the realization he was still holding on to her arm.

He let go and she missed the contact immediately.

He turned back to his book and Mary finally let out a breath she didn't know she was holding. He had proven that he needed her company, that she could help him. She focused herself back to her story, thinking about those long fingers, and the desperate way he wanted her to stay.

The Prince's hands were wrapped around his Mistress' breasts, length grinding into her backside. She gripped the shelf in front of her, the pantry's musk clinging to her throat.

"Please let me have you." he moaned in her ear. "You have tortured me long enough." He ran his tongue up the side of her neck. Heat filled Mistress at his blatant need for her. The Prince had not yet earned her attention, had not yet proven himself.

"I have done no such thing." She replied, reaching backwards and squeezing his member. He let out a tortured groan. "Take out your need on one of your other women." She spat. Mistress would not be a play thing for a pompous prince. He grunted and flipped her around, leaning forward to touch their foreheads. He grabbed her

hand in his and pressed it against his chest.

"There is no other woman in here." He said, his eyes tortured.

"Prove it." She ordered, turning around and exiting the small pantry.

Mary smiled at the boldness of her Mistress. She had never been confident enough to assert herself to anyone, let alone a man. Mary truly was non-contrary.

Would she want to assert herself against a man?

Would she enjoy feeling powerful and important? Mary rolled her eyes at her own musings. Of course, everyone would want to feel powerful and important.

"You can sit here again next time." a gentle voice offered. She glanced up to her table mate, watching him as he packed up his belongings. "If you want."

Mary didn't let herself relish in the idea of what depraved things her animal brain wanted, but her ethical human brain definitely wanted to help the quiet man.

She just had to figure out how.

5

As usual, Mistress stepped into her bed chamber after supper. What was not usual was the basket placed on her bed. She peered inside tentatively, carefully inspecting the contents. She extracted a modest bundle of flowers.

They were beautiful and delicate.

Her callused hands and dull nails were a depressing juxtaposition.

She placed them in a vase on the window sill and returned to the basket, grabbing the remaining object inside - a linen wrapped brick.

Mistress carefully unwrapped the cloth revealing a fragrant soap. Royal soap, Mistress knew. She had haggled with the merchant herself the week before. Mistress held the soap up to her nose, inhaling deeply. The fragrance was deep and complex, and reminded her of the Prince's skin.

She hung the strip of cloth on the mirror of the vanity.

It would serve as a visual reminder of her luxurious man when the pangs of loneliness were the most intense.

Mistress longed to run her nose against the crease of his neck, to taste his pulse point again.

It would be easy for her to grab a washing bowl and run the soap over her skin, to paint an illusion of what she could be. Is this what the Prince wanted? To pretend that she was not one of the struts on his throne, holding him as he sat in comfort. Did he think it would be so easy to wash away her common skin for his benefit? Disappointment and a pang of anger filled her chest. The Prince would not tell her what she was or needed to be, regardless of his power.

Sadness ached throughout Mary's limbs, causing a pause in her writing.

She felt the Mistress' pain and doubt. She knew what it was like to feel less than, like she had to mold herself to be something to someone. Mary refused to let her Mistress live in that way. Mary still struggled to understand what her role would be for her new table mate.

What did he need from her? She wasn't sure what shape she should mold herself.

"Are you a writer?" a familiar male voice asked. Mary looked up from her notebook and threw a smile at him. His face was relaxed but blue eyes were serious. Mary's smile wavered slightly.

"Definitely not. I'm a snot wiper, mostly.

From play equipment, not faces." she clarified. He nodded, eyebrows furrowed and
returned to his book. He looked handsome
when he was serious, sharp lines becoming
even sharper. Perhaps he needed her to be
the fun silly friend to get him to lighten up
a little.

"Are you a reader?" she asked, a coy expression on her face. Certainly he would understand the joke and let out a giggle, Mary
would have been satisfied with a chuckle.
Alas, his eyebrows remained furrowed.

Okay, so he didn't need a jester.

"Recreationally. Professionally, I write software." he replied. Mary nodded, both in response to him and in understanding of his
character. His shy disposition made sense.

Mary had befriended many shy boys in her childhood, the boring often being drawn to the plain. While they lacked social skills, usually they were nice enough. Unfortunately, they also didn't bathe enough but this man looked very clean so far. Clearly, there was more to him that she would have to unravel. The image of unraveling his lithe frame from a cocoon of silk sheets infiltrated her mind, causing a pang of arousal to hit her core. Mary combed her fingers through her hair, attempting to smooth away the salacious thought. If this man was a programmer he definitely did not own silk sheets. He probably had a star wars bedspread, not sexy at all. Unfortunately the image of him bound and gagged on-top of a graphic of R2D2 did nothing to cool the heat building within her. Mary shook her head, resolving to distract herself instead.

"What else do you do, recreationally?" she inquired, voice shakier than expected.

"I work a lot, no time for much else." he answered with nonchalance. Her heat instantly cooled with concern. It would explain how tired and hungry he looked, and Mary didn't like it. Everyone deserved rest, even shy library acquaintances. This strengthened Mary's resolve to shelf her lust, this man needed a friend and counsel.

Mary nodded empathetically. "I've heard the tech sector can have brutal hours. Your job must have some PTO, at least." she offered. His eyes softened at her answer, face relaxing. Mary's heart soared at his reaction, glad that he responded well to empathy and validation, as it was something she could definitely provide him. Mary's veins thrummed with satisfaction at being able to help him, even just for a moment.

"My boss is a hard ass, but I'll see what I can do." His eyes danced and mouth pinched, like he was keeping a secret.

Mary wondered if his boss was similar to hers, with the jarring insistence of time off. Unfortunately, the dark purple that surrounded his eyes made her believe otherwise. Maybe she could convince her new friend to go to the spa with her, he clearly needed some relaxation. They could get those couple massages, but as friends of course. Would they have to undress in the same room? Mary's face heated at the image of his long fingers undoing the buttons of his shirt. Would he let out moans as the masseuse pressed on his tense muscles? His shoulders must be sore from all of that hunching. Mary could also give him a massage, she was a fast learner. The image of her prince whimpering under her touch caused a sharp prick of desire in her groin. Perhaps better to let the professionals handle it.

Regardless Mary felt resolved to nurse her sweet new acquaintance back to health.

A loud knock reverberated against the door. Mistress smirked as she opened it, moving to recline on her bed. She laid slowly, relishing in her power.

"You think this is funny?" the Prince spat, waving the parchment wildly at her. The veins of his forehead pulsated with anger, haggard breaths stretching the silk of his blazer. He looked delicious when he was this angry.

"I'm not certain I understand, your majesty." she lied, tilting her head coyly. He sneered and shook his head. The Prince walked back towards the door and Mistress sat up, suddenly faced with the potential he may walk through it. The Prince turned the lock swiftly and walked back to the foot of the bed, causing her breath to halt. His glower left Mistress wondering if perhaps it

would have been better if he had left.

"No, I am the one that does not understand. I do not understand why I came to my bed chamber as usual after supper only to see every working girl in the city sitting there. Imagine my surprise to find I had apparently personally summoned them!" He waved the letter around again, forehead veins continuing to pound.

Mistress rolled her eyes. "Hyperbole. There were only five." she replied, crossing her arms.

"Five too many!" he exploded, his eyes were intense as they bore into hers. Her loins heated in response, gaze flicking down to admire his tense frame.

"You looked wound up, I figured you could use the release." she explained, reclining back once again. She had to remain in control.

He took a deep breath in an attempt to calm himself. He walked over to the vanity, placing the parchment on the worn wood. His eyes shifted to the opulent linen hanging from the mirror. His posture softened at the recognition of the cloth: the fabric that was wrapped around the soap he had attempted to gift her. He was bewildered to find the loaf of grease sitting on his breakfast plate the next morning, unsure where he had went wrong.

"First you return my gift, and now you give me an unwanted one." he mused, running the satin between his fingers. "Why refuse such a generous luxury but keep the scrap that cradled it?" he wondered aloud, deep in thought. She crept off the bed walking behind him, grabbing the cloth from his hands.

She tied the fabric around his head, obscuring his vision. The Prince's breath caught for a moment, resuming with an increased rate. This aroused him, she noted internally.

"This scrap shielded the soap on its journey, protecting its delicate scent and valuable body." she murmured, stepping to the front of his frozen frame.

She trailed her hand around the circumference of his waist as she walked, maintaining contact the entire time.

He shuddered against her palm, deprivation of sight heightening sensation.

"Perhaps the soap would not be where he is today without the protection of the scrap. Sometimes value is not so easy to judge, wouldn't you say?" she teased, running her hands up his abdomen

and around his head. She pulled gently, coaxing his face closer to hers.

"Perhaps the soap should show a little gratitude to the scrap...with his mouth." she instructed, taking a step back without letting go of his head. He followed without hesitation, letting her guide him. She briefly removed her hands only to place his palm on her thigh to anchor him as she perched herself on the vanity.

She lifted her dress and her thighs opened, "Show me your gratitude, Pet." she ordered, watching him intently.

"Yes, Mistress." he groaned and fell to his knees, face burying into her core. His skillful tongue caressed and probed at her folds, bringing overwhelming pleasure quickly. The Prince knew her intimate folds well, and he demonstrated it with

finesse and speed as he brought her to climax. When her shuddering ceased she removed the cloth from his face. He squinted at first, adjusting to the light from the window behind her. In that moment it was easy to pretend that she was the sun that was blinding him with her brilliance, an outlandish fantasy for Mistress to entertain. When his eyes adjusted he laid his head on her thigh, calming his own ragged breaths. She played with his hair gently, admiring the dark locks.

"It was a beautiful soap. You shouldn't waste it on me." she finally said, her voice small. It was better saved for his royal skin, or the body of the wife he would inevitably be assigned. She would remain here regardless, haggling for the next batch. Her bravado had faded with her desire and now she was left with insecurity.

"I was a fool to think I could woo you with a hunk of grease, no matter how pretty." he murmured, eyes closed in relaxation. "I should thank you for the unorthodox lesson. No one has ever challenged my mind or body in this way." he continued, a peaceful smile on his face. Mistress certainly hoped that was true. The thought of him begging for anyone else soured her gut.

"Although, I don't understand the role of the prostitutes in this lesson." he said, finally looking up at her. His eyes were a clear and soft lapis, it caused a stirring in her heart.

"Maybe I was hoping for a break from your unrelenting harassment?" she joked but her words rang hollow. In truth, Mistress needed to test if the Prince only came to her out of sexual deviance, and to show him how she could and did

coordinate the world around him. She chose not to tell him this, best a lesson he learned on his own.

He gave her a wicked smile. "Oh, I'm only getting started." His eyes blazed, lips placing open mouth kisses on her inner thigh. Heat began to stir in her core once again. Mistress smiled and threw her head back, allowing herself to hope.

Mary closed her notebook with finality, the aching in her center too strong to bear. She caught the eyes of her table mate as she stood. His gaze lingered on her flushed cheeks for a moment and Mary swore she saw a spark of need in it.

"Excuse me." she mumbled and escaped to her usual single stall hideaway. She shook her head as she walked, ridding herself of the wishful thought that her handsome friend may think of her in that way.

Mary felt jealous of the power Mistress had over the Prince, how she could so easily play sexy games with him. She stayed hidden during the day, attending to his needs in secret while relishing in his sensual devotion in the bedroom.

Mary couldn't think of anything more desirable than that dynamic.

She hastily locked the door and shoved her hands into her panties, as she had done the previous day in this bathroom. Her thoughts drifted to her muse as they always did, this time inspired by the blindfolded Prince of her story. She imagined taking his tie and wrapping it around his tired eyes. Her fantasy self went further and shoved the currently soaked panties into his panting mouth. Mary paused her rubbing for a breath, surprised by her own depravity. She had never considered herself a kinky person before, she'd never even orgasmed during intercourse. She couldn't let herself get lost in pleasure while in the presence of another, couldn't open herself to that sort of rejection. She usually squeaked and squawked how her partner liked and took care of herself after. She was lost to pleasure in that bathroom, picturing handsome lines of his face and expressive eyes. Unexpected shudders began when she envisioned her muse flushed and needy while she blinded and gagged him, saliva running down his chin.

"Oh, god." she whimpered quietly, unable to help herself. Just as she crested over the peak, a knock bounced off the door.

"Um, are you okay in there? You've been gone awhile." The worried voice of her friend was muffled behind the door.

Mary was still convulsing when she attempted to answer.

"One-one second please," she stuttered

through the descent of her high.

"Are you sure? You don't sound so good. Are you sick? I know CPR, I think." he questioned, tone still strained with concern.

Mary laughed quietly, partly from his adorable concern and partly from the afterglow of her orgasm. Mary opened the door without further thought, still slightly dazed.

"I'm fine." she reassured him, but quickly realized her mistake.

His worried gaze inspected her for harm but lingered on her flushed cheeks and damp brow. His eyes widened in surprise as they drifted down to her clothes that were still askew from her passion. Understanding dawned on his face and was followed with a tint of pink to his cheeks.

"Oh, I'm sorry." he mumbled and walked back to his seat, head tucked down.

Mary closed the door again and freshened up in the sink. Her movements were stiff and robotic, consumed with panic. She pondered the expense of funeral arrangements, as she would surely pass away from embarrassment.

Fortunately her friend appeared calm and collected when she returned to the table.

He greeted her with a smile and wave as she sat in the chair across him, opening her notebook as usual. Mary longed to return to the world of a Mistress who didn't doubt or embarrass herself, who was bold and smart and everything Mary wasn't.

The Prince threw a silk vest towards his Mistress as he strode into her room. Mistress looked up from her knitting, posture still casually reclined. The vest was beautiful, with ornate embroidering just to his Majesty's liking. It was, however, several sizes too small.

Mistress smiled smugly.

"I know what you're doing." he hissed with accusatory eyes.

"You want to play games of power. Show me that every part of my life is in your hands." He spat, gripping his vest and holding it in front of him for emphasis. Mistress swallowed, her mouth suddenly dry. She had been relishing in her games, enjoying how he flustered when she meddled with his meals, social engagements, and most recently clothes. She had been patient-

ly waiting for any recourse or consequence. He could easily have her executed or banished for treason, but he had simply suffered in silence. It was intensely arousing.

"I've had enough!" he exclaimed, throwing down the vest with such force her shoulders jumped. "You have been tormenting me for weeks with this nonsense." He slowly placed his knees on the bed, climbing on and crawling towards her. The fury in his gaze was slowly melting to intense need.

Fear and excitement mixed in Mistress' core.

"You have been torturing my mind with your games, while denying my body." he purred as he stalked closer. "I can take no more of this. You will have no playmate because I will have gone mad." He reached her feet, sitting back on his

haunches. He took a foot in his hands, caressing it gently. His gaze softened, shifting down to where his hands were working.

"I will accept your lessons with gratitude, but teach my body as well. I will be your obedient slave, but I need just a sliver of you in return." he said, looking back up at his Mistress. His eyes were needy, the bulge in his pants pronouncing how true his need was. Mistress could feel her own need pooling in her panties, but now was not time for her pleasure.

"You will come to my room every evening after supper, and our games will not leave these walls." she vowed, slowly creeping her free foot towards his straining cock. He moaned and glanced down, watching her foot rub the length of him.

"I think you can wait one more day for relief."
She removed her foot. The Prince suddenly collapsed backwards on the bed, letting out a long miserable groan.

Mistress smiled and began to plan.

"Jesus Christ," her library friend mumbled. Mary glanced at him with a raised eyebrow, a brilliant grin still planted on her face.

"I'm going to need sunglasses if you don't cut that out." he continued, covering his eyes as if blinded. Mary glanced around the room. The lights were very much fluorescent, or more likely LED. This particular area had not one window, so no need for eye protection. He must have noticed her confusion because he quickly explained, "That smile was at least a thousand watts." he finished, a pink tinge to his cheeks. Mary had a feeling he knew that it was ultraviolet radiation that caused eye damage and not the rate of energy transfer.

"Was that a pick up line?" she asked, a coy

smile plastered on her face.

"You have a pretty smile, is what I'm trying to say." He lowered his gaze, bravery running out. She couldn't stand to have him doubt himself, at least when it came to her.

She reached over and grabbed his hand. "Thank you, I think you're pretty handsome too." she cooed, gaze soft when he finally raised it off the table.

He let out a sharp humorless laugh.

"Okay, you don't have to go that far." he said, pulling his hand back. Mary's heart deflated, disappointed he did not believe her. It was time for her to turn up the love and support. Purely platonic love, of course.

"I'm serious! You're a handsome young man,

probably have several ladies awaiting your beck and call." She batted her eyelashes in jest. Mary was determined to make him smile again, she had more conviction in this than anything else.

He rolled his eyes.

"I'm thirty eight, hardly a spring chicken, and even if I did, I wouldn't know how to talk to them." he explained, eyes remaining steadfast on the book in front of him.

Mary was surprised at both his age and his dating hesitation. Well, she wasn't surprised that he was shy but certainly was convinced someone would have captured his fancy. A hot bolt of jealousy ripped through her at the thought of him being intimate with anyone else. Mary dismissed the pesky

emotion quickly, it was completely inappro-
priate for the context. He was a new friend
she was attempting to uplift, the last thing
he needed was her barking like a dog at nearby women.

No, this was not about Mary.

"You've been talking to me with no problems
so far. Plus, talking isn't always necessary,
you have pretty eyes." she offered, hoping
to boost his confidence and make him smile
again.

He gifted her with a shy grin.

"I don't think I could stop you from talking
if I tried." he teased, grabbing her hand that
was still outstretched. He inspected it with
his eyes and fingers, tracing the lines of her
palm. His expression grew somber.

" I, uh, had a stutter when I was a kid, got made fun of when I tried to make friends. I guess I just stopped trying." h e shared, her heart ached for him. She imagined him as a child with floppier hair and a smaller nose. Mary knew what the pain of rejection was like, knew the devastating consequences it could have on someone's self-worth.

"Well you're my friend and didn't even have to try!" she exclaimed brightly, attempting to exude the happiness she wished he would have.

"I had to try very hard actually, but thanks." he said quietly. She continued in her quest to raise his self-esteem, determined to coach him to a happy and fulfilling life.

"Plus you don't need to be likable to get girls.

How have you gotten laid in the past?" she asked, attempting to find a new angle for her pep talk.

His hands paused and face became bright red. She didn't know he could go that color.

"I haven't."

6

Mary couldn't stop thinking about their last conversation as she set up her pen and notebook. How on earth could a man at his age be a virgin? Even ugly people had sex. Even ugly, smelly people had sex. She lost her own virginity in high school, but granted all she had to do was open her legs and seem agreeable.

Maybe he was born with a deformity and

had no dick. It would explain why he would feel shy engaging in romantic relationships, most women needed a penis to be fulfilled sexuality. Mary pondered if she needed it to be fulfilled. She had enjoyed penises in the past but mouths and fingers were also perfectly adequate.

"Do you have a penis?" she blurted without thinking. His bravery and openness was rubbing off on her. She started thinking about him rubbing something else off. She imagined the pale skin of his face flushed, his head thrown back in ecstasy. She imagined his whimper as he tugged on his cock. Oh god, how she hoped he whimpered. The room suddenly felt very warm. Either she was going into early menopause or required chemical castration.

Her prince let out a strangled cough. "Last time I checked." he answered, wide eyes glancing around the mostly empty library.

Okay, so he had the tackle. Maybe the rod just couldn't perform?

Her first boyfriend had performance anxiety and couldn't maintain an erection to save his life, it did save her virginity at that moment. He ended up having a pee fetish so Mary was grateful. Erectile dysfunction was also common in men as they aged. She made a mental note to search for the pathology of erectile dysfunction when she got home. She shook her head, her muse was likely too young for that particular condition. Another possible cause was religion, she knew several girls in her graduating year that saved themselves for marriage. The very devote ones asked her to lay underneath their bed and shake it while their boyfriend inserted himself. Mary always thought it was strange that God was blind to thrust less intercourse.

"Are you catholic?" she questioned, scanning his frame for any religious memorabilia.

His eyes narrowed in suspicion. "You're trying to come up with an excuse for my chastity, aren't you?" he accused, placing his elbows on the table and leaning forward. Mary sputtered for a moment, unable to come up with a response. No one had ever caught on to her inner ramblings before.

His bright laugh floated across the table and

settled straight into Mary's chest cavity. She was quickly becoming chemically dependent on his happiness.

"Don't waste your cute little brain cells," he said, leaning back and picking up his book again. His posture was relaxed, face serene. He seemed so much more relaxed around her compared to the first day, causing satisfaction to tingle up her spine. Mary watched him idly as she collected her thoughts. It shouldn't matter to her why he held on to his purity for this long, clearly his inexperience affected his confidence.

Mary believed that dwelling on the past was a waste of time, but changing the future was her obligation.

All the pieces finally snapped together in

Mary's mind. That was why she was so un-usually attracted to him; the universe was telling her she needed to help him enter sex-ual activity. There was no better person to help him. Mary's nonjudgmental mind and tolerant soul were perfect for the task. She would build up his confidence with her sup-port and launch him into the dating world dick hard and ready to experience life. Mary chose not to think about where that would leave her.

She admired his subtle mannerisms that she had grown familiar with. He often sat with one leg crossed on top of the other, switch-ing them periodically. He also had a bad habit of chewing his nails, particular during a tense scene in his book. Mary glanced at his short stubby nails and winced. She didn't know how he could tolerate having them like that, one hangnail ruined Mary's whole week.

Mary felt a pang of sadness when her friend slid his book into his bag. She considered asking him to stay longer, when her phone rang.

The vibration hammered against the table from inside her bag. Mary hurried to answer it.

"Excellent news, Mary." her boss said, Mr. M didn't waste any time with his phone calls. "Your unpaid vacation is being extended another week."

Mary's breath caught. Her friend met her gaze, concerned look indicating he could hear the conversation.

"What about the center?" Mary asked, dumbfounded. She couldn't imagine the man was wiping up boogers himself while she was away.

"Esmeralda's sister offered us the opportunity to start a disabled dog rehab program in Guatemala and I simply could not refuse. Surely, you understand?" he explained. Mary decided she didn't like Esmeralda's sister, although clearly she had some connections.

Mary took a deep breath to steady her disappointment.

"Of course, sir." She swallowed her rising anxiety at being jobless and turned up her empathy. "This is a great opportunity, I'm sure it'll help your healing. Good luck." she responded, a genuine smile on her face and in her voice. They said their goodbyes and Mary tucked her cellphone back in her bag.

"You're too nice," her friend accused with narrowed eyes.

Mary laughed and shook her head. "There's no such thing as too nice."

The intense look he shot her devastated her resolve. Was there a thing as being too nice? How could being understanding ever be a bad thing?

"It's dishonest. Someone could disregard and hurt your feelings because they don't know how you really feel about it." he argued. Pain shot through Mary's rib cage at the thought of being perceived as dishonest. Mary would rather stand on a bed of nails than hurt anyone's feelings.

"Bold of you to assume anyone has ever cared about my feelings." she retorted, the newly formed crack in her logic armour causing a stray emotional reply to fall out. People were usually too busy riding the high of her praise to think about her intentions. Not her prince, apparently. His eyes widened for a split second in surprise before dropping to his fidgeting hands.

Silence stretched between them for a long moment.

"I could probably find you some work to do." he offered. "It wouldn't pay much, though."

Mary smiled but shook her head.

"That's very kind of you, but I'm not very

technically savvy—I would be a handicap." she admitted sadly. She would love to be able to see him more, but couldn't accept a job she was unqualified for in good faith. He laughed suddenly, the accompanying warmth to her chest a welcome reprieve from the tension.

"Don't worry, the technical positions are filled. This would be a..." he paused for a moment to consider something. "...clerical role."

The warmth lingered in her chest. It was nice having someone try to help her for a change.

"I do know my way around an email." She smiled genuinely. "I can send you my resume, but be warned my Excel proficiency is an extreme exaggeration." She reached over to her bag but his hand was suddenly on top of hers.

"Not necessary," he interrupted. "Your character reference is compelling." His hand and gaze were warm, fueling the heat in her chest.

She could get used to having a friend.

Mary wasn't sure whether to be happy or scared.

7

Mary yawned as she sat down in the now familiar plastic chair. She had stayed up too late browsing job boards for possible quick cash jobs. She believed her friend when he said he would try and get her temporary income, but Mary had never been able to rely on anyone and she wasn't going to start now. Her sleep had not been peaceful, dreams filled with kind blue eyes and flushed cheeks.

Mary did not do well with uncertainty, in fact she molded herself to every situation to prevent uncertainty. Even if the world was going sideways she could always count on herself to be right side up. Her friendship with the prince was quickly shifting, and Mary was desperate to understand what her role was.

Did he need a friend to show him that making mistakes would not hurt him? Yes, Mary was certain of this.

Did he want more than that? She recalled his attempt at flirting, and the few heated looks he gave her. Mary chewed on the end of her pen, deep in thought.

Did he want more only because she was a safe person? Mary was pretty convinced he cared about her since he offered to get her a job, but did he only offer to be kind? Mary now understood what her friend was saying about the dishonesty of overt kindness. Mary rubbed her temples in mental exhaustion. She opened her notebook, hoping that maybe her Mistress' kinky antics could distract her.

The Prince was sitting at the vanity, chiseled features reflected in the mirror. He wore exhaustion openly, eyes fatigued. Mistress was combing his hair, brushing the soft locks back and revealing high cheekbones.

"What troubles you, pet?"

"Politics." he dismissed, clearly uninterested in recalling his work.

"Too complicated for a lowly common girl?" she teased, playfully pouting into the mirror.

His blue eyes met hers in the reflection, not an ounce of humor in them. She stopped combing, pushing his hair back with her hands to inspect his face. He averted his gaze from hers.

"What's happened?" she demanded, gripping his chin with one hand and his hair with the

other. The Prince was usually full of fire, it was distressing to see him extinguished. The contact seemed to comfort him as he finally spoke.

"I've been matched to a wife." he said with the theater of a funeral March. Mistress' heart paused, she was unsure if it would start again. Regretfully the intense pain in her chest indicated it did restart.

"Oh." she breathed, still processing the implications of his words. His eyes were broken, dark with misery. She released his head, hands sliding down and resting on his shoulders. The luxurious fabric of his blazer felt rough on her fingertips.

She swallowed her heartbreak and said, "Congratulations, your Ma-"

"Don't," he interrupted her. Mistress was glad

he did, as she was not certain she could finish the sentiment without shattering at his feet.

"Why did you come here?" she asked, uncertain what he wanted from her. Did he need a last screw before leaving her forever?

"There was nowhere else for me to go." he said truthfully, his eyes pleading for comfort, for her direction.

She was strong, and right now he needed her.

She swallowed her misery and spoke, "Nothing has to change. You will be king and no one will question a mistress."

"You are not a mistress, you are my Mistress!" he exploded, rising to his feet. Mistress felt relieved that the internal fire she loved was not fully quenched.

She cradled his face in her hands.

"How long do we have?" she cooed, pressing their foreheads together. He let out a defeated sigh and squeezed his eyes closed.

"Early negotiations still, likely several months." he explained, groaning softly as Mistress began stroking his hair.

"Then there is no use fretting. Tomorrow may be uncertain but today, right now, I'm here." she reassured, planting a soft kiss on his lips. He deepened the kiss, desperate to lose himself in her. Mistress was happy to oblige him.

"Up." she ordered, wrapping her arms around his neck. He grabbed her bottom and hoisted her up, walking forward and pressing her up against the wall. His tongue pressed into her mouth with intensity, searching for hers. The *hardness pressing into her center begging for her. She wrapped her legs around his waist, purposely grinding on his clothed erection. He groaned into her mouth, the sound feral and wounded. His lips trailed down her jaw and neck, nipping their way towards her shoulder. He thrust against her, letting out a stream of moans. Mistress had never seen her Prince like this, so raw and vulnerable. It was at that moment she realized he had given her his heart to look after, and she would cradle it with care.*

"You are good and right and nothing can change that." she praised him through panted breaths. He mewled into the crook of her neck, tears landing on the skin of her collar bone. "My Prince will remain strong, because he will break only for me." she demanded, clutching his head and shoulders desperately. His thrusts sped up, pres-

sure increasing to her clit. Mistress was very close, but could not go over without him.

"Break for me, pet. Give me your release." she ordered, going over the crest of her orgasm in time with his. Slowly they returned to the safety of the ground. She continued to stroke his hair as he softly wept in her arms. Mistress would do anything for the Prince, that was the only truth she was certain about.

Mary shut the notebook, body and mind heated. She trudged off to the bathroom, needing to clear her head. The cold water she splashed on face caused goosebumps to cover her skin. Sadness filled Mary as she thought about Mistress and the Prince. She commended her for putting aside her own heartbreak to take care of the Prince when he needed her.

Would he find it dishonest that she put on a brave face for him?

Mary shook her head.

Putting your needs aside to help others was honorable and good. Mary didn't know much, but she was confident in that. It certainly didn't hurt when helping others included embracing a handsome man.

Would Mary's prince let her hold him like that?

Mary's body hummed with pleasure at the thought of being the caretaker of his heart and body. Mary resolved herself to chase the pleasure of helping him, dishonesty be damned. She would spend this week inflating his sexual ego and prove to him that letting people in would not hurt him. That was enough for now.

She returned to the table relaxed, head and heart cleared.

Mostly.

"I have something to confess to you," her friend began, face concerningly serious. He looked like he was going to announce a death or debilitating disease. Mary's heart

picked up pace. Perhaps this was the reason for his abstinence, a horribly disfiguring
venereal disease. Mary felt an avalanche of
sympathy for him, assured that she could
learn to love him regardless.

"I've been reading your story while you're
in the bathroom." He admitted, eyes cast
downward in shame.

She blinked.

That was not what Mary was expecting.
Suddenly self conscious of her spelling and
grammar, Mary thought a venereal disease
might have been easier to accept.

When she continued to gape at him, he continued to speak. "You're normally so calm I
just needed to know what could possibly get
you so flustered." he admitted, "And well,

now I just can't help myself." he blushed, gaze dropping. "I know that it's a horrible invasion of privacy, and I am so sorry, and you are my friend now, but it is very good-" he continued to ramble, ringing his hands nervously.

Mary's face and core heated. He was interested in her story. Mary imagined her friend reading through her note book, lips parted and face flushed in arousal. The Mistress would make him read the entire notebook aloud from start to finish as punishment. His hands would be tied behind his back, forcing him to turn the pages with his mouth. Heat exploded inside Mary, imagining his mouth and slobber anywhere near her. Hope glimmered inside her that his interest was more than academic.

"Are you um, into that?" she asked, interrupting him.

"Irrevocably breaking the trust of my closest
friend? No. I feel like shit about it actually-"
he continued to spiral.

"No, the, uh, contents of the story."

He paused to contemplate.

"You mean, would I like a woman to be that
way with me?" He looked up, seeming to
consider the question deeply. Mary waited
with bated breath, her anticipation camou-
flaged under a calm facade.

He was quiet for a long moment.

"I don't want to say the wrong thing and
make you think I'm a lunatic." he said hon-
estly, unable to look at her.

"Don't worry, I'm also a lunatic. I've learned that unless it's at work or a funeral it's better to just say it." Mary reassured him, she was still reeling from him referring to her as his closest friend. Friends with benefits was a thing, she was pretty sure.

Her soft voice and reassurance pulled his eyes back down to hers. "I think I would like it if you did it." he admitted, his gaze unfocused. Her core clenched and burned. The world around her spun, disbelief pounding through.

"Why?" Mary could not believe that he wanted her in this way. Plain non-contrary Mary, a sex object? It couldn't be believed.

"I'm not good at knowing what people expect from me. I guess being told exactly what to do and being praised for it sounds appealing. Simple. You're my friend and I trust you, but I don't want it to be weird." he started back pedaling, doubting himself again.

He trusted her. Honor filled Mary's chest at being given such a gift. She had no choice now but to foster and nurture that trust he gave her. She was so desperate to ease the worry of her prince, she cast her raging libido aside.

"It doesn't have to be a sex thing. There are other ways for you to please me." she said with a smile.

He quirked an eyebrow.

"The point is just for me to make a request, and you to accomplish it. Let's start with

something small, but with consequence."
she said, looking around for inspiration. She
attempted to channel her Mistress, to get
into the mindset of a domme. Her muse was
picking at the spine of his book, long fingers
tipped with haggard nails. The smile that
slid over her face was lithe.

"I want you to paint your nails." she stated, her eyes meeting his with assurance. His
eyebrows raised, clearly surprised at the request.

"I don't have nail polish."

"That's not my problem, and if your nails
aren't painted by the end of the week, it
will be your problem." she explained, voice
and face remaining happy and pleasant. Her
body thrummed with excitement.

Would her prince really allow her to make demands?

Would he follow them?

"My problem?"

"If you're a good boy there will be a reward, if not..." she explained sweetly, trailing off with what she hoped was a threat. He shuddered at her words, Mary suspected it may be from the praise. She would have to test it out at a later date. Mary relished at being able to test out anything with him, adding another layer of ways she could comfort him.

"No sex?" he asked, eyes hesitant. He was clearly maintaining the friendship boundary and Mary was happy to respect it. More visits to the relief stall may be in order.

"Not even first base." she smiled, attempting to hide her small disappointment.

"Okay."

Now she had to figure out literally everything else.

8

The next day, her prince's nails remained bare.

She had spent the majority of the night planning all the potential choices and outcomes her friend could make. Despite being excited to dole out punishments and rewards, Mary didn't want to rush him into making a choice. She opened her notebook, satisfied with getting lost in the sexy antics of the

Mistress.

The Prince was late. Mistress smiled to herself, perched at the vanity once more. Her orders were very clear: he was to be in her room precisely one hour after supper. This meant the Prince was currently half an hour in arrears. Excitement bloomed in Mistress' chest and loins as she pondered the consequences of the Prince's indiscretion. She held her eyes closed, concentrating on this task. There was no knock this time. Mistress heard the soft open and close of the door and felt a warm set of lips pressed against the back of her neck.

"You're late." she stated. She turned around in her stool, disengaging his arms from around her. She missed the contact immediately, but there were important plans ahead.

"Oh, I was just -" he began but she didn't let

him finish. She unfastened his pants and pulled out his hardening cock. His mouth opened in surprise, heat quickly filling his eyes. Miss held his handsome cock in her hand, tracing the path of the veins and ridges. By the time she lavished from root to tip, he was fully hard and shaking in her grasp.

"Miss, I-" he began. Once again he was interrupted when she slipped the tip between her lips.

"Oh, Jesus." he groaned, a dab of his essence landing on her tongue. His pleasure was delicious, causing Miss to let out a little moan.

"More, please, Miss." he pleaded. He immediately realized his mistake when she looked up at him sternly. "If-if it pleases you." he stuttered. Power and pleasure radiated through her. She took him deeper to reward his amendment.

"Oh Jesus. Yes, thank you." He moaned, his head tilting back and eyes pressing closed.

She continued to suck and bob, his responding groans growing frantic. Just when she felt his scrotum twitch she froze and released him.

"Miss, I was so close." He cried, his breath ragged.

"I know, pet." she cooed, lips just grazing his tip as she spoke. To demean such an important man with an informal name was thrilling. Power radiated through her veins, fueling her boldness. "Delay is frustrating, isn't it?" she purred, stroking him once. Understanding flashed through his eyes, this was a punishment and not a reward.

"I'm sorry, Miss." he apologized, his eyes desperate but earnest.

"For what, my sweet?" she asked, giving the head of his cock a chaste kiss. He jumped in her hand, demanding more attention.

"F-for being late. I-" he began to explain. She lifted her hand to silence him.

"I'm not interested in excuses. You may beg for my mercy." she said, voice remaining cool. Her loins were on fire, demanding his capitulation.

"I'm so sorry, Miss. I'm sorry for wasting your time. Please, please forgive me." he pleaded, his whole body shaking. She took his cock back in, bobbing slowly and evenly.

"Thank you for your kindness, Miss. I won't disappoint you again." he gasped. When his balls contracted this time, she let him come. When he finished, she stood and pressed their lips together, letting him taste his release. He moaned *softly, eyes remaining close after the kiss.*

"You are forgiven." She murmured. Wrapping her arms around his trembling frame.

9

On Wednesday morning, Mary caught a flash of light blue as he opened his book. Excitement and small disappointment washed through her. She was worried he would make this choice. She came prepared.

"Well done, pet." she praised, trying out the nickname. His returning smile was heated, he really did like praise. She inspected his hands and noted that he was meticulous, not one speck was missing or in excess.

"I'm going to be honest with you, I had to retry several times. It's not as easy as it looks." he admitted, smile shining with pride. Her heart sang, she had never seen him be proud of himself.

"You should always be honest with me." she agreed, shifting her mind back to the lesson. "Do you understand why I asked you to do this?"

He shook his head.

"Do you see what a beautiful color this is?" she asked.

He nodded.

"It would be a shame to ruin such a beautiful

color with your teeth."

His eyes softened in understanding, and slight confusion.

"Why does it matter if I chip them?" he asked, gazing down at his hands.

"Women are very sensitive, you can't very well touch them with sharp, chipped nails." His gaze shifted between his blue nails and the inseam of her pants, swallowing audibly.

"Yes, of course." he grunted. Mary's core tingled at his inspection. She steeled herself for the next step, summoning bravery. She was the Mistress, strong in her convictions and sure of herself.

"Why did you pick blue?" she asked casually,

already knowing the answer. He narrowed his eyes at her slightly, as if she was an exotic creature he was trying to understand. At that moment she felt exotic, smart and powerful.

"Because it was the least-" he didn't finish, clearly struggling with the right words.

"The least...?" she prompted.

"Um, girly." he breathed out, suddenly aware of his mistake.

"Hmm, I feared as much." she stood up, grabbing a paper bag from her backpack and placing it in his laptop bag.

"I put a pair of my underwear in your bag." she began, zipping up his bag. They were not especially sexy panties, plain bikini cut cotton. They were very much feminine, with pink flowers and hearts printed on them. "You are going to wear them all day tomorrow. Work included." she instructed, stopping behind his seated frame. She braced her arms on the table at either side of him, bringing her mouth to his ear.

She slid the reward into his novel, a 'don't worry be happy' bookmark she had purchased the day before.

"You did well, pet." she murmured, praise earning a responding shutter.

"But you can do better."

10

Mary was first to the Library on Thursday morning, an unusual event. Her mind began turning to find an explanation for the deviation, refusing to believe she had scared him off with her request. He could be sick, everyone got the flu sometimes. Mary had swine flu in highschool and had gone to school regardless to avoid her mother being called for an absence. She had started a low carb diet so was a wee bit fragile at the time. Mary remembered reassuring her mom she was fine and not to worry, despite being very much not fine. Mary shook her head, disappointed in her past dishonesty. Suddenly there was a new pressure in her chest, was she unfair to her mother?

Did her mother deserve to know the truth, despite the possible consequences?

A gentle throat clearing interrupted Mary's musings.

She looked up to see her prince, sitting in the seat across from her. He was tense, eyes cast downward. Mary was so distracted she hadn't noticed him, a first for their friendship. She scanned the tables around them, pleased to see that they were alone for now. She reached forward and grasped his hand, tracing its lines and ridges with her fingertips. The contact seemed to relax him, his shoulders dropping a few centimeters.

"How was work?" she asked, hoping he would understand what she was implying. His eyes flickered up to her for a split second before returning to his hands.

"Hard." he said, truth in his voice.

"Look at me." she instructed gently. His eyes met hers meaningfully this time. He wore embarrassment plainly. Mary knew this was a possibility, but didn't think it would affect him this much. She didn't think he seemed particularly misogynistic, but then again they'd only been speaking for a couple weeks.

"Were you a good boy?" she asked, tone remaining gentle.

He nodded, eyes glancing away from hers in embarrassment again.

"Can I see?" she asked, motioning to pull down the waist of his pants so she could inspect the top of his undergarments. He cleared his throat nervously.

"I took them off. They require laundering." he explained quietly, eyes steadfast on the floor. Mary held back a smile, her poor embarrassed prince. She was disappointed that she didn't get to see evidence of his submission. The image of him sitting at a computer in her undergarments was the star in last night's fantasy. At that moment, his person-

al growth was more important. She interlaced their fingers.

"Don't worry about it, I have plenty to
spare." she reassured, pleased to see him
soften under her compassion. "Do you understand why I asked you to do it?" she asked
softly.

He nodded confidently, eyes steadfast as
they held hers.

"Because I picked the most traditionally
masculine color. I assumed that is what I
was supposed to do, instead of asking you
what you wanted." he answered, clearly he
had been thinking about this.

Mary's eyebrows raised, she was not expecting this response. She had assumed he
picked blue due to fear of ridicule and possi-

bly fragile masculinity. Of course he would act based on societal norms instead of his own wishes. Mary felt exceptionally stupid for her oversight. She did still have some confusion about his embarrassment.

Why would he be so distressed if it was not due to masculinity related issues?

Mary narrowed her eyes in focus.

"And what did the punishment teach you?" she enquired, aware that her intended lesson was significantly different than what he understood.

"That you're still the boss, even when we're apart." he answered quickly, face flushing and eyes heating. Mary's skin felt hot in response to him. He thought she asked him to wear her panties as a reminder that he belonged to her. Mary closed her eyes and steeled herself, tamping down the deep ache in her core. This was not the time to thirst for this perfect man. Mary vowed to add this moment to her spank bank for later. She was Mistress right now, stoic and strong.

Mary still could not account for the embarrassment he wore so blatantly when he arrived. He clearly was not bothered by the nail polish or the punishment. Mary suddenly remembered that he was late today, which was highly unusual.

"You come here straight from work, right?" she inquired, slowly beginning to understand the series of events.

He nodded, lips downturned and eyebrows furrowed in confusion. "Yes, why?" he asked.

Mary's smile was sly.

"So if you had to remove any article of cloth-ing, it would have had to be here." she be-gan, resting her chin on her hands coyly. Mary could sense his growing unease. "So that article of clothing would likely be in your bag, yes?" she continued, nodding to-wards his laptop bag. His gaze immediately dropped to the floor, embarrassment return-ing. "I would like to take them, since they are mine." she finished carefully, not wanting to push him too far too quickly.

He did not speak for a long moment, gather-ing his resolve.

He took a deep breath.

"They're dirty."

Mary rolled her eyes.

"I have a dad, it's not like I've ever seen a skid mark befor-"

"I came in them." The words rushed out of him, eyes squeezed shut. It looked physically painful for him to admit that.

Mary's mouth popped open in shock.

She wasn't expecting this.

Mary usually hoped for the best and expected the worst, but this was better than she could have ever hoped for.

"Why?" she asked, genuinely curious. Many men had panty fetishes, the taboo can be quite arousing. Mary once had an ex boyfriend that would steal all his female friends lacey thongs and wear them in secret. When she found out she made him return the stolen articles and bought him his own.

He leaned forward to whisper, "Because I was sitting at my computer for 8 hours thinking about your pussy." His face had never been so close to hers. From this distance she could see the inner circle of his iris was actually a much darker shade of blue than the rest. His eyes were wide, suddenly conscious of their closeness. If Mary leaned forward even a hair she could press her lips with his. Is that what he wanted, or was she just clouded with infatuation for him? Mary lost her nerve and leaned back.

"I thought you didn't want this to be a sex thing."

"I never said that."

Mary paused, remembering their previous conversation. He was right, she had assumed. Mary was disappointed in herself, her mother had taught her 'when you assume you make an ass out of you and me.'

"Do you want this to be a sex thing?" she asked tentatively, trying to keep her face and tone neutral.

"I um, well," he struggled, unable to meet her gaze. He cleared his throat and squeezed his eyes shut. "If it pleases you."

Mary had never felt such an intense wave or pleasure and happiness at his words. Her smile was full and brilliant. He was a very quick learner.

"You've definitely earned your reward, then."

She leaned forward and placed a chaste kiss on his pale cheek. His skin was warm and smooth beneath her lips. "You are a very good boy, and I am proud of you." she cooed against his skin.

"Thank you." he murmured when she returned to her seat, fingers grazing where her lips had just been. He had a dazed look on his face, a light flush colored his usually deathly pale skin, and his shoulders loose with relaxation. He was devastatingly beautiful and wanted to be hers. At least in a domination and sex way. Mary's veins hummed in excitement at the added possibilities if she could involve his penis in their games. A penis he had never used for this purpose before.

Mary had to be careful going forward, this was all uncharted waters for him. He put a lot of trust in her to unfurl his maidenhood, he deserved her full attention. Mary couldn't help but imagine him laying in a bed full of rose petals, ready to be taken. The arousal she had previously tamped down reemerged, causing dampness to pool between her legs. It was now her responsibility to teach him how to enjoy his sexuality, it would only make sense for her to use herself for demonstration.

Mary's chest filled with conviction and excitement, by the time she finished with him his penis skill would cause her to scream his name!

Mary was painfully aware at that moment that she didn't know his name. He wore her panties but she didn't know his first name.

"What's your name?" she asked.

"Oh, um, George."

She couldn't help but let out a laugh. His face transformed into confusion.

"I've always thought you look like a prince, it's fitting you have such a royal name. " she explained, his face breaking out in a radiant smile.

"I will accept that, considering most of them were diseased and inbred." he teased and joined her laughter.

Her prince was George.

11

"Open wide, pet." Mistress instructed, placing the ball of chocolate in the Prince's mouth. He complied and moaned as he chewed. The Mistress repeated her action twice more with a grape and a slice of apple. She was sitting with her legs outstretched and parted comfortably, feeding her Prince.

*"Please, no more, or you'll have to fetch the car-
riage just to get me down the hill." he pleaded,
stretching out on the cotton blanket and resting
his palm on his taut stomach. The sun bounced
off the opal buttons of his undone shirt. The
Prince looked relaxed, inhaling the valley air
with easy breaths. He had convinced mistress to
accompany him to the fields to assess the possibility of planting sunflowers next season. He
then led her straight past the crop fields to the
patch of long grass that overlooked the river. He
surprised her again by pulling out all the supplies for an impromptu picnic from his canvas
bag.*

It was nice.

*Mistress didn't dare hope for future repeats.
His upcoming nuptials were hanging between*

them, tension increasing weekly.

"How are you feeling?" she asked, hoping to avoid more thought on her own feelings.

"A bit warm, actually. Do you have a fan hidden somewhere in your dress? I require cooling." he joked, wiping the back of his hand on his damp forehead.

Mistress rolled her eyes, and reached over to grasp one of the water glasses. She dumped the cool liquid on his chest without hesitation, earning a shriek from the Prince.

"Hey, what was that for?" he asked, sitting up abruptly. The newly wet shirt clung to his chest, rivulets of water trailing down towards the tidy trail of hair above his groin.

"Being a pest." she replied, unable to keep her

eyes from his half naked and now damp form. The Prince noticed her gaze, face lighting up with mischief. Mistress did not like this at all. He slowly rolled to his knees, crawling over to her. The Prince on his knees had not yet lost its appeal, an ache now pounding deep in Mistress' womb.

"An act of assault on the future King," he began, adding a haughty lilt to his voice. Mistress narrowed her eyes, a playful Prince meant trouble. "I could try you for treason right now." he continued, crawling forward until his face was mere centimeters away. "But you are no common criminal," He breathed, eyes raking the length of her body. His close proximity heightened her arousal. "I know a witch when I see one." he said, his arms braced on either side of her. She was trapped both physically and men-

tally by him. "Do you know what we do with witches?" he asked rhetorically, licking his lips.

"Drown them." he answered, grabbing the entire pitcher of water and dumping it over her head.

"Ack!" she sputtered and gasped, pushing her now soaked hair out of her eyes. Before she could even open them, his lips were crushed to hers and she was pushed onto her back. They were a flurry of hands and need, wet clothes being removed and landing in the tall grass loudly. He thrust inside and groaned in relief. She clenched around him, arousal allowing him to be fully seated. They sighed in unison, relaxing into their embrace. He braced on his elbows, their chests pressed together.

"Free me from this charade." he groaned as he

began thrusting slowly. "I cannot sit through one more council about marriage alliances."

Mistress moaned, wrapping her legs around his waist, urging his thrusts faster.

"Please, witch. Take me away." he begged into the crook of her neck. "Wave your wand and turn me to a toad so I can travel in your pocket."

His thrusts grew frantic, hitting Mistress in a place inside she had never discovered before.

"But please don't kiss me. Please keep me forever." he pleaded, pushing up onto his palms, watching her face as she crumbled beneath him. His words and cock were overwhelming and she screamed for him, climaxing without abandon. He silenced her with his kiss, emptying himself inside his Princess.

Mary put the pen down, breaths more elevated than she expected. She looked up to see George's eyes on her. They flicked back down to his book, pretending as if he didn't get caught looking. Mary chuckled and pushed the notebook towards him, now that she knew he was interested.

George put his novel down and grabbed her notebook, shooting her a small smile of gratitude.

Mary watched him read several lines, swallow, close his eyes and push the notebook away.

"I can't read this in front of you." he confessed.

Mary frowned.

He cleared his throat and motioned towards his crotch.

"Oh…" Mary's mouth formed a small o in understanding.

Her face and center heated simultaneously. She leaned forward further, trying to see evidence of this erection.

"Hey!" he snapped and covered his lap with his book. "Don't look at it!"

"Why not? It is rare and untouched. Likely unseen. Maybe I want to study it for the sake of scientific discovery?" she joked, pretending to look through invisible binoculars.

He didn't laugh at her light-hearted attempts, in fact his eyes were sad.

His face dropped, fingers began to pick at

the spine of his book. "I'm worried." he said, shifting his gaze to the floor. A pang of hurt sliced into her gut at his change in mood. She couldn't handle his self-doubt.

"I don't think I will be able to satisfy you, sexually." he finished, unable to meet her eyes.

"Considering we are sitting in a public library I was not expecting you to." she replied, trying to ease his concerns with humor. She didn't understand why he would suddenly be so concerned about satisfying her, unless it was tied to him getting an erection.

"Why, is it small?" she leaned forward, trying to sneak a peek at his groin again. She didn't consider that his equipment was simply too small to be functional.

He cleared his throat again, visibly nervous. "Perfectly average, thank you." he took a deep breath.

"But the problem is I don't want to make a mistake and disappoint you." he fiddled with the spine of the book as he talked, careful not to chip his polished nails on the binding. Regardless of the reasons, at that moment he needed her reassurance.

She giggled and covered her hands with his. "You seem awfully concerned with something that hasn't happened yet." she cooed. He paused and finally lifted his gaze. It was soft and warm, much like his hands underneath hers. "The only way you could disappoint me is by not being true to your-

self and what you like." she continued softly. "Plus, the science shows that making
mistakes makes someone more likable." she
spouted, unable to restrain herself. His face
transformed in that moment, determination
now taking over.

"Right." he confirmed. Suddenly he pulled
his hands out from underneath hers,
grabbed her shoulders, and pressed their
mouths together. It was sloppy, inexperi-
enced and frankly not very good.

It was perfect.

They pulled apart just as suddenly, panting.

"Right." She repeated.

He grabbed his bag and walked out the
doors.

12

Mary was in a crisis of epic proportions. She liked George, like, a lot. Mary liked George more than she'd ever liked anyone in the past. Now that he had kissed her, she gave herself permission to initiate the next step.

She spent the entire weekend trying to figure

out how she could ask him out.

"Hey, friend. I liked kissing you, and talking to you. Can we do both of those in a different location?" she whispered to herself as she walked from the bus stop. She shook her head and tried again.

"Good afternoon. I know that I've already made you wear my panties as a friend but perhaps you could wear my panties as a boyfriend." No, this was not about the panties. Maybe she should leave the word friend out of it entirely.

She was just pondering the sexiness of the word comrade when she reached the front doors of the library. She spotted a piece of paper stuck to the glass with clear tape.

Closed for yearly maintenance

Her stomach sank. She would have to wait for another day to embarrass herself.

Maybe they were installing carbon monoxide detectors.

Just when she was about to turn around and head back for the bus, she felt arms encircling her from behind. She smelled a familiar soap and instantly knew it was her prince.

"We're hugging now?" she teased, covering his hands with hers, basking in the feel of his touch.

"You told me to do what I wanted, and I don't want to disappoint you." he said against her cheek. Her loins tightened at his words. His need for her validation was stirring an ache deep in her belly. She could feel his breath on her face and its tempo against her back.

"Looks like the library is closed." she stated, turning her head to look into his eyes. They were squinting, trying to read the sign.

"It appears so." he confirmed, straightening out and untangling himself from her. Her heart cried at the loss but recovered when he interlaced their hands together.

"We're holding hands?" she gaped.

He was still studying the sign and attempting to peer through the glass. She continued to gape. This must be a hallucination. She probably got hit by a car on the walk here, this was the side effect of her brain's sudden and tragic demise.

"Of course. Come on, I live across the street."

he began walking, using their clasped hands as a leash. He led her precisely eighty four steps to his apartment, up the elevator and through the door. She was stunned into silence, which was an amazing feat. It wasn't until she had a cup of water in her hands and was sitting on his couch that she regained the function of her frontal lobe.

"Wait, why do you go to the library to read if you live across the street?" she asked. He was sitting a respectful distance away, his legs crossed and arms open on the back of the couch. At some point during their journey he had released several more buttons from his shirt and mussed up his hair. It was in that particular moment that reality sunk in to her. She was in his apartment. Alone. He could murder her and no one would know her last location. He would be a patient seri-al killer, that's for sure. He didn't really seem like the cannibal type, she'd have to inspect his freezer to make sure. Most serial killers had mommy issues, she regretted not ask-ing about his relationship with his mother. Mary felt a pang in her gut when she realized that George would probably be the only per-son to notice she was gone.

"I spend all day sitting in my office alone. It's nice to be around humans I'm not financially obligated to talk to. Even just for an hour." he answered, looking out the large windows of his living room. The space was neat and simple, like him. There were no overwhelm-ing smells or colors. Mary felt comfortable here, like it was where she belonged. It prob-ably had something to do with the fact that

George turned his head and gazed at her with adoration.

"That makes sense." she nodded, lowering her gaze to the cup in her lap. If he kept looking at her like that she may pass out and she really was not in the mood to test out if he did, in fact, know CPR.

Eventually he sighed and stood up.

He grabbed the cup from her hands and placed it on the coffee table, kneeling between her bent knees. This put their faces on equal level, he gazed at her in an attempt to read her mind. Oh Jesus, he was looking at her and kneeling between her legs. She slowly visualized every Catholic pope in descending order, a pathetic attempt to prevent her from jumping his bones. Just when she reached Pius XI he spoke again.

"I've been thinking about what you said, about doing what I want. You're right, I haven't been true to myself. I guess I'm just used to doing everything wrong. " he said quietly. A pang of sadness sat in her chest. Who could make such a thoughtful man feel so unsure of himself?

Unless of course he did turn out to be a serial killer.

"But I'm not worried now, with you. I want to spend time with you, as my friend. " he said softly, smiling at her. Her heart sank slightly at his words. She did want to be his friend, but her wanton thoughts would be a challenge to control. She was making a plan to look up chastity belts online when he continued to speak.

"I want more than that too." he insisted, a hopeful look in his eyes. "I should have asked before I kissed you, I'm sorry. You just make me feel so bold and I want to kiss you and touch you and please you." he placed his hands on her knees, gently massaging them. She felt heat pooling between her legs. Mary was still in disbelief that a whole human being would want to be devoted to her pleasure, Plain Non-contrary Mary.

"But why? You barely know me." she managed to breath out. His blue gaze was boring into hers, warm and relaxed. He seemed comfortable like this.

"I know your name is Mary, I know you take the bus everyday even though there's a driver's license in your wallet," he started. When she raised her eyebrows he quickly added "It fell out of your bag last week."

He started absentmindedly rubbing her knee. "I also know that you're kind, and patient. When Mrs. Lee comes to drop off her books you help her put them in the bin and offer to grab her new ones from the holds section." he continued, looking down once again. Whatever he planned to say was difficult for him. She missed his eyes immediately.

"I know you're the most beautiful woman I've ever seen. I know that I like the way you smell, and I like how you say everything that's on your mind exactly when it gets there. I know that I've been thinking about our kiss nonstop, and more." he said, breath quivering with nerves. He took a deep breath.

"Like how I wish I made you look like that when you opened the bathroom door. " he finished quietly, his words hesitant but earnest. Mary was transported back to the moment she opened that door, the flush of her orgasm still on her skin. Her heart melted at his words. He wanted to please her, he just lacked the confidence. His honesty gave her the bravery she needed.

She grabbed his chin and tilted his face up to look at her. Her prince, her George, wanted her. Most importantly to Mary, he needed her.

The air in the room became incredibly hot

and thick.

"I'm going to kiss you now. You're going to take my lead. What I do with my mouth you're going to copy, okay?" she instructed. She felt his tension in her grip as she relayed instructions. It must relax him when she took control.

"Do you think-could you call me Miss when we're together like this? It might make it easier to stay focused." she continued. She could be braver if she wasn't Mary. He nodded his head slowly, his breathing getting heavy.

"Yes, uh, Miss." he replied, heat sparking in his eyes. Her sex clenched, he was intoxicating.

She slowly pressed her mouth to his. She

teased his lips open with her tongue, demanding entry. He willingly gave in and began teasing her tongue with his. It was very erotic, but she was running out of air. She pulled them apart suddenly, both of them panting.

"When you need a break you can trail kisses on my neck and chest, I will do the same." she demonstrated. He let out a quiet groan when she licked and nipped at his Adam's Apple. When she returned to his mouth he mirrored her previous actions. The feel of his lips and teeth on her neck was intensely pleasurable. Heat radiated from her neck down to her chest, causing her nipples to pebble.

"You can touch my breasts as well, with your

hands or mouth. The nipples are particularly sensitive, so be careful." she instructed, her breath becoming suspiciously pant-like. His mouth began to descend down her sternum, his hands covering each breast. She leaned back to give him better access. He placed open mouthed kisses on her breast overtop of the thin shirt, nibbling at the nipple gently. Need flooded to her core. If they didn't stop now she would jump and ride him before he was ready.

"S-stop." she managed to breath out, using every drop of willpower remaining. He immediately pulled away. His face was flushed and his eyes were dilated. She had never seen a more erotic sight.

"Did I do something wrong?" he panted, his

eyes worried. She smiled softly and held his face in her hands.

"No, pet. You did very well. Too well. I don't want to get carried away." she explained. He took a deep breath and nodded. Slowly he stood up, bringing a significant bulge in his pants into her view.

A mischievous smile crept up her face.

"I see you have a situation." she said, pointing at his erection. Somehow his face flushed even further.

"Um, yes. I'm sorry." he mumbled, looking at the floor. He gripped his cock, partially to obscure it, partially for the pressure she suspected.

"Never be sorry, but you better take care of it.

Right here." she tapped on the couch cushion next to her, urging him to sit down. He hesitated for a moment. She needed to give him reassurance.

"I want to watch you stroke yourself. It would please me to see you come." she clarified. This seemed to put his mind at ease. He sat next to her as instructed and pulled out his erection. It was average in size as he had claimed. Uncircumcised, with a large bulbous head and thick shaft. It made her mouth water. She stood and sat on the coffee table in front of him, allowing for a direct view of his work.

"Touch yourself, pet. Like you do when you're alone. I want to see you come." she purred.

He swallowed hard and placed his long fingers around his shaft. Slowly he pumped up and down, lingering on the head. Droplets of precum coated his fingers. She wanted to lick them away. Instead she climbed on top of his lap, looking down at where his hand still rested on his cock.

"Keep going, I want to see." she encouraged him. He began stroking again, remaining near the head. It was very intimate, watching him pleasure himself between their bodies. Mary closely observed his technique and preferences. Her breaths in sync with his, it wouldn't have surprised her if their heartbeats were also aligned. He groaned quietly as he worked himself, throwing his head back with eyes shut tight. He reached his peak quite quickly. They would have to work

on that if she was going to orgasm during intercourse. His seed painted his hand
and shirt, and Mary could not hold back her
hunger any longer.

She lifted his hand to her mouth, licking the
remains of his semen from it. His lips parted,
eyes watching her intently. The heat in his
gaze was boiling despite the recent orgasm.
When his hand was sufficiently clean, she
rested her head on his shoulder, taking several deep breaths to calm her racing heart.

"You are going to be the death of me." he
whispered.

"No," she murmured back. "My mother is a
nice lady."

13

George was quiet during dinner, she got the sense he wasn't used to this. He was usually quiet when he was second guessing himself.

"Have you ever had dinner with someone?" she asked, trying to distract him from any self-doubt.

"Not someone I wanted to impress, and I

usually forget to make one at all." he answered, taking another bite. His gaze was trained steadily on his plate.

"Well, you're in luck. I'm rusty on my table etiquette." she laughed and placed her hand on top of his. "Relax."

He looked up at her and smiled. Her heart melted.

The conversation flowed easily. She learned that he was an only child and that his parents both worked at a bank. They kept to themselves but were nice enough. In turn she told him about her own parents who were divorced but happily so. She worked hard to keep their peace, making sure not to cause too much trouble growing up. She told him stories of her father working late, giving her ample opportunity to watch shows she was too young for. They laughed when she relayed how her mother didn't know how to use the BBQ so Mary became proficient by the age of eleven.

"Who took care of you?" he asked, loading their dishes into the dishwasher.

"Well, my parents did. I didn't starve or any-thing, I even got a new iPod when I sent mine through the laundry. Twice." she handed him a fork.

He shook his head. "I mean, emotionally. Whose shoulder did you cry on after your first breakup? Who busted you smoking in the bathroom?" He closed the dishwasher and leaned against it, crossing his arms. She pondered for a moment.

She shrugged. "I guess I just didn't need that." she said, turning to wash her hands in the kitchen sink. Mary never really thought about anyone needing to take care of her. She was a perfectly capable young woman, she certainly didn't need a caretaker. Plus, helping others in need certainly felt much more rewarding. The image of George looking up at her with adoration as he kneeled at her feet gnawed at her.

Was that what being taken care of felt like? Mary certainly liked that. She felt arms encircling her from behind, dipping into the waistband of her pants.

"I'm sure I could find some ways to take care of you." he purred against her neck. One of his hands palmed her breast while the other parted her damp folds. Mary moaned at the trail of fire his fingers left. Mary could get used to this new bold George, she regretted not telling him to be true to himself earlier.

"Holy fuck, you're wet." he said, tentatively dipping into her heat.

He paused for a moment, unsure. He wanted to please her, to make her orgasm. He had no experience and there was no sense of expectation from her. No matter what she did or asked for, she would not be rejected. A weight lifted off of Mary's soul, allowing her to lose herself in the sensations, in George.

"Just make sure to focus on my clit and you'll be fine." she breathed, head lolling back. Her throat was open to him and he took advantage. He lathed open mouthed kisses to her neck and shoulder, nipping occasionally. His tongue was eager and wild against her skin. Heat started building in her womb.

"Oh, Jesus." Mary moaned. He pressed two fingers into her, the slickness allowing easy entry. His other hand slipped into her panties, flicking her clit rhythmically. He certainly had good instincts. He continued to pleasure her with his hands, the combination of internal and external stimulation overwhelming her quickly. The assault of pleasure from his hands and his mouth on her neck brought her to the precipice.

"George, I'm-" she stuttered out, gripping onto his arms for strength. Her knees were weak and shaky.

"Yes. Please, baby. I need your come." he

purred in her ear, maintaining his speed and increasing the pressure on her clit. The combination of his pleading and casual endearment pushed Mary over.

Stars exploded behind her eyes as she convulsed in his arms. She was going to fall in love with this man. George brought her down from the high slowly, eventually slipping his hands out of her underwear, straightening her clothes.

Her post orgasm trance was broken when she caught sight of herself in the hallway mirror.

"George, what the fuck is this?" she demanded, inspecting the large purple and red mark on her neck.

"Looks like a hickey to me." he said, glancing

at it with satisfaction.

"No, George, this is a disaster." she panicked.

George's face dropped. "You're mad. I'm sorry. I've never given one, I thought that's
what couples do-"

Mary didn't hear a word he said, too busy
catastrophizing.

"I work with children! I can't just go into
work with an announcement on my neck
that I had sex!"

"Technically you didn't have sex-"

"George!"

He laughed, resting his chin on her shoulder.
"You've still got another week off, so don't

worry about the job stuff. I got you, remember?" he squeezed her waist. Mary's heart
quivered.

George had her. Heart, body, and soul.

"You heard back from your boss?" she asked,
head a little woozy from his earlier declara-
tion.

He nodded with a coy smile.

"Pass me your phone, let's give him a call."
he requested. She obliged and watched quietly as he dialed the number.

To her disbelief, George's phone vibrated in
his pocket. She snatched her cell phone back
and hung up.

"You're the boss?" she asked, already knowing the answer.

"Sort of." he shrugged. Mary paused and contemplated this new development. Relying on this man she just met for an income would be risky at best and idiotic at worst. She glanced at his reflection in the mirror, his warm blue eyes dancing with hers. If there was any man she could rely on it would be George.

"I don't think it's ethical to sleep with your employees." she stated, trying to sound apprehensive about this deal.

"Technically we haven't slept together-"

"George!"

He sighed.

"You would be the only employee so the nonexistent HR department wouldn't hear of it."

"The only employee? What exactly do you do?"

"I make and sell software for commercial chemical sensors. You know, like fire alarms or-" he began.

"Carbon monoxide detectors." she finished.

14

Geroge's office was an office. It met the technical specifications for a work-place, and not much more.

The carpets were gray, the walls were gray. There was a desk, a handful of gray chairs, and two doors. No art on the walls. The one positive was that it smelled clean. One of the doors led to the bathroom, the other she assumed was his personal office. The desk was piled with various papers and other stationery supplies, computer monitor obscured by file folders.

"No wonder you work from home so much, I'm already depressed." she said, running her fingers across the dusty parchment.

"I'm not exactly the decorating type." he mumbled, clearly embarrassed. Mary was compelled to reassure him.

"Well," she took a deep breath, "let's see what we can do, shall we?" she smiled, and his answering smile was all Mary needed.

Mary spent the entire day organizing and attempting to decorate the office. George gave her a very generous budget for supplies and she made good use of it. The good thing about gray is that it matched everything.

By Friday, the desk was bare and the reception area was at least eighty percent less depressing. That left Mary with the conundrum of how else she could make herself useful.

She knocked on the door of his office.

"You don't have to knock." he laughed softly.

Mary smiled and opened the door. He was sitting at the desk, typing quickly. When his eyes lifted to hers, her breath caught.

"Hi." she said, suddenly forgetting what words to say.

"Hi." he replied back.

"What do you want me to do now?" she asked, leaning against the door jam.

He leaned back in his chair with hands tucked behind his head, looking up in deep thought. The fluorescent lights bounced off his cheekbones, highlighting just how much he'd changed since that embarrassing day in the library. His cheeks were fuller and under eyes considerably less purple.

"Hmm, I guess my emails could probably be organized. I should be signed in on the reception computer." he suggested. She nodded and turned back, desperate to find a way to still be useful to him.

To say his emails needed to be organized was an understatement. He had 2,465 unread emails, none of which were junk or spam. No wonder he was so stressed and tired. Mary took a deep breath and got to work. Mary separated his emails to different folders, and flagged urgent ones for George to answer.

They had lunch in his personal office, Mary perched on his desk.

"You need another person. No one could possibly do all this by themselves!" she said as they sipped from their mugs. Hot chocolate for her and tea for him. He nodded sheepishly, looking down at his hands.

"I guess I never expected it to be so much. I thought writing the software and troubleshooting would be it." he admitted, eyes still cast downwards.

"At this pace it would take you ten years to fill these orders." she said, finishing the last few sips of her drink. "Those clients are not going to stick around forever, and the stress is going to give you cardiovascular disease."

He continued to nod somberly but didn't say anything. She stood up, and walked over to him. She lifted his chin, forcing his gaze up at her. His eyes were blue and needy.

"It's a good thing you're not alone anymore." she smiled softly, pressing a kiss to his forehead. George didn't smile back at her, his blue eyes drifting back to the hickeys on her neck. Mary recognized the look of guilt in them, it was one she was very familiar with.

"George," she began, grabbing their empty mugs and placing them on the desk. "You know I forgave you, right?" she murmured, cupping his face in her hands. His gaze remained steadfast on her neck, teeth gnawing on his lip.

"You shouldn't have." he said quietly, truth clear in his words. He truly believed he did not deserve forgiveness. Mary had a few ideas for solutions.

"Do you need a punishment, pet?" she asked, increasing the pressure of her hands on his jaw.

He nodded.

Mary carefully undid several buttons of his shirt, revealing his firm chest. George watched her hands as she moved, eyes curious and heated. She began to place deliberate open mouthed kisses to his skin, sucking firmly.

He moaned loudly. "I wouldn't call this a punishment."

Mary laughed against his chest, continuing her work. By the time she was done with her mission, George was panting and shaking against her mouth.

She leaned back and admired her art. George's chest was now decorated with a large purple M, the top extending past where he typically buttoned his shirt, so Mary could still see evidence of her mark when he was all put together again.

Mary smiled with satisfaction, "Now we're even." she said, hopping down from the desk. Mary could have left it at that, but she knew that George needed to suffer to absolve himself of the guilt. She recalled that he came in his pants just from wearing her underwear, so clearly he had a weakness for her undergarments. She quickly slipped her panties off and balled them in her hand. George's eyebrows raised in surprise but his eyes remained heated.

"Open." she instructed, tapping on his bottom lip. "Good boy." she praised when he complied. His teeth were straight and eggshell white, either he had braces or was genetically gifted.

She shoved the panties into his mouth. "Get back to work, you can take them out when we leave."

Without another word Mary walked out of his office and returned to her desk.

By the end of day Mary had successfully attended to 10% of the emails on his behalf, tailing each response with her new email signature labeling her his 'executive assistant'. Her bare ass on the gray faux leather chair was a constant reminder that her prince was nearby, probably suffering. Suffering for her. The thought ticked Mary's loins and heart simultaneously. She was just about to open another technical support ticket when she heard his footsteps behind her.

For the first time since she'd met him, George was standing with no hunch in his back. Mary looked up at him from her desk chair, she could confidently guess he stood at 5 feet and 10 inches. Another part of him was also standing very tall, but Mary chose to ignore it for now. The panties were still balled up in his mouth, his eyes looked almost vacant, like he was somewhere else. His skin was flushed, and she could see streaks of redness where his saliva had sat on his skin while he worked. His shirt was soaked with it, becoming transparent enough to faintly see the hickey initial on his chest.

He was an erotic masterpiece that Mary didn't know she could create.

She ignored the infernal blaze in her core, her prince needed some care.

Mary stood and flattened her palm in front of him, signaling the punishment was over. The fabric dropped from his mouth, fully saturated with his saliva. She carefully slipped the wet undergarments on, relishing in the depravity of his slobber on her most intimate place. He watched her with precision, face still blank. She carefully led him into the bathroom, grabbing a hand towel from the shelf. She sat on the counter to improve access to his face. She carefully cleaned him up, intermittently peppering his cheeks and chin with kisses. She tucked his forehead into the crook of her neck, embracing him and running one hand through his hair.

"You are a good boy and I am so proud of you." she murmured tenderly. She continued to praise and pet him until eventually he raised his head out of her grasp.

"Thank you," he whispered, kissing her deeply. His face was still flushed and tender, but his eyes were no longer distant, simply lethargic. "Let's go."

Mary was brimming with pride, pleased at her competence and ability to help her prince. Her boyfriend. Was he her boyfriend? So far he was her friend and submissive. Mary suddenly realized that he may not be interested in her romantically at all. They never really talked about it, just slipped into new roles that revolved around each other.

Did she want him to be her boyfriend?

It wasn't until he had pressed the button on the elevator of the apartment that she gathered the courage to ask.

"What are we?" she asked.

"Riding in the elevator." he answered. She rolled her eyes and smacked his arm.

He laughed and wrapped his arms around

her waist.

"You are my salvation, and I am your help-less servant." he said, nibbling on the side of her neck. She laughed and pushed him off. Silly George was new but she liked him.

"I'm serious! How should I introduce you to people?" she asked, wrapping her arms around his neck. He pressed their lips to-gether softly.

"However you like, sweetheart." he said be-tween kisses. He began to trail his kisses down her neck to her cleavage. She ignored the fire burning in her sex.

"Oh, hello. This is George, my boss slash sex slave." she imitated, breathing becoming la-bored from his attention.

"I think we have firmly established that you are the boss." he murmured against her nipple that he was currently nibbling on. She rolled her eyes again. Clearly, he was not capable of serious conversation when he was drunk on his desire. His hands drifted to her ass, needing each cheek firmly. Mary let out a small moan, gripping the back of his head.

Panic began to build in her belly at how weak he was beginning to make her. He could easily shatter her completely and she couldn't do anything to stop it.

Luckily the door to the elevator opened, saving his virginity for the time being. They separated suddenly, panting loudly. He grabbed her hand and led her to his apartment.

"Come on, there's work to do."

For the first time Mary started to believe that perhaps he was not the only one that needed help.

George was sitting on the end of the couch, fingers tapping furiously as he worked. Mary let her eyes roam his figure, appreciating the strength and severity of his features. He wore sweatpants and a t-shirt at home. She vaguely remembered him mumbling something about "no dirty clothes on the couch". He never made any comment about her clothes, but regardless she changed into shorts and a tank top when she arrived. The smile he gave her was worth the extra trouble.

Mary opened her notebook, prying her eyes away from her George.

"I brought you a gift." The Prince said. Mistress looked up to see an open jewelry box in his hands. "I beg you not to return this one with prostitutes."

The necklace was large and opulent, it did not belong on her common skin.

Mistress shook her head.

"It will be a scandal."

"So let it!" he exclaimed, clearly exasperated by her continued objections.

"And how will I live with myself if you lose everything because of me?" she pleaded, losing the fight to remain strong and unaffected.

"How will I live without you? I cannot. I cannot

keep living this lie that my heart and soul is still my own." he retorted, desperate for a way to show the world that they were two halves of the same whole.

Mistress had an idea, desperate to ease the heartache of her love.

"Give me the necklace." she stood up and placed the chain around his neck, fastening it swiftly.

"Now the whole world will be able to see it, but only we will know its significance. You will be able to feel its weight and remember that you're mine." she cooed, wrapping her arms around his neck. His gaze was heated and the groin of his pants firm between them.

"I'd rather wear your legs around my neck, but it'll do." he grumbled, but devotion shone in his eyes.

Mary felt sympathy for the Prince, she was also struggling with being only one facet of George's life. However, she didn't let herself even consider becoming a permanent fixture of his life– it would be a selfish act. The pleasure would be immense, she had to admit. George had managed to see into her more deeply than any other person ever had, which was just as frightening as it was thrilling.

Mary looked up at George, carefully studying him. His shoulders were now raised, a curve to his upper back. Mary glanced up to the square analog clock above the TV. He had been working for several hours, clearly he was becoming fatigued. His typing remained furious, no sign of stopping to rest. He needed his Miss.

Truthfully, she needed the distraction of her Pet.

Mary stood. The notebook fell to the floor, causing her prince to look down at it. His gaze then lifted slowly up her bare legs and ended at her stern brown eyes.

"Pet." she said sternly.

"Miss." he replied, his gaze trained on hers. He understood they were in their lesson.

Mary shifted herself and sat in the corner of the couch, parting her legs.

"Lay here while you work." she instructed. He hesitated a moment but complied. He switched from the laptop to his smartphone for comfort. His furious typing resumed, including the tension in his shoulders. Mary pressed one hand to the spot where his neck met his clavicle. The other hand planted firmly in his hair. She ran her hands softly through the silky strands, earning a moan of pleasure. His head was sensitive. Mary smiled to herself.

She bent forward to whisper in his ear, "If I feel you tense up, I will pull." she demonstrated, tightening her hold on his head. He gasped at the new sensation, but relaxed his shoulders.

"Keep working." she instructed, and resumed softly stroking his hair. He needed her reminders approximately every ten emails, consequently letting out a sharp breath and a moan each time. Mary's center heated with each moan. By the 3rd pull, the aching was unbeatable. It didn't help that she could clearly see his erection, the sweatpants doing nothing to hide it from her view.

"Have you ever eaten a pussy, pet?" she asked. She felt him stiffen between her thighs.

"No, miss." he answered.

"Would you like to?" she asked.

"If it pleases you." he replied. She could sense the truth in his words, but the hesitancy as well.

"Come here and look at me." she instructed. He placed his phone on the coffee table and flipped over, bracing his hands on either side of her. His gaze was worried when it met hers.

"Don't worry, I won't let you fail. Just do what I say and I will be very, very pleased." she purred. His eyes heated and body relaxed. She pulled his shirt up and off his body, revealing his firm chest. She could see the goose flesh that pricked his skin. When he was situated back between her legs she began her instructions.

"Kiss my pussy and inner thighs." she commanded softly. He placed soft chaste kisses to her inner thighs and panty clad labia. It was sensual and infuriating. Their game had been a sufficient warm up.

"More pressure. Open your mouth and use your tongue." she said, holding the back of his head gently. He obliged, and was rewarded with a rush of slickness to her sex. The grit of his fresh shave pressed against her, leaving a trail of fire behind him.

"Please, Miss." he whimpered.

"Please, what?" she inquired, breathing now slightly elevated.

"Please let me taste it. It smells so good." he moaned, trailing the outline of her panties with his tongue. Heat shot to her core. Her prince knew exactly what to say to arouse her.

"Yes." she panted, disappointed with how unsteady her voice already was. She laced her fingers through his hair, in attempts to guide him. He wasted no time pulling her panties to the side and diving in. He was enthusiastic but unfocused.

"The top. Suck and flick my clit with your tongue." she ordered. He obeyed with unexpected finesse. He was a very fast learner. She was embarrassed at how close she was getting so quickly. He continued to lathe her clit with his affection. The sight of her prince between her thighs was almost too much to bear. She looked away from his tongue lapping at her, attempting to gain control. It was then she noticed his hips gyrating.

"You're fucking against the cushions, baby. Does eating my pussy make you hard?" she asked, hoping to distract herself away from climax.

"Yes, Miss." he confirmed, between licks.

"Tell me about it, Pet." she commanded.

"It's the taste," he panted. "And the smell. It

feels so good on my face. So warm and wet. I want you so bad." he continued between mouthfuls of her cunt.

This was too much.

"You're going to make me come, Pet. You're doing such a good job." she moaned, her legs trembling. She felt his body shudder.

He liked praise.

"Do you want to drink down your Miss's come? Beg for it." she panted, vision blurring.

He groaned against her core.

"Yes, please. Please, miss. Please give me your come, I need it. I will take it all, I promise. Please, give it to me." he pleaded, sweat dotting his brow. She was a goner.

She felt the beginning of her climax burning through the soles of her feet.

"Look at me, look at your Miss while she comes in your mouth." she breathed out. Once his blue eyes looked into hers, the waves of her orgasm finally crashed over her. She was vaguely aware of her prince swallowing repetitively, as her slickness gushed out. His hips were still gyrating wildly. He stopped his assault when her contractions eased, careful not to overwhelm her. He was more astute than he gave himself credit for. He rested his cheek on her hip, waiting for her next instructions. She suspected he was also attempting to calm down, the gyrating of his hips had stopped. When her breathing had sufficiently calmed, she began stroking his hair again.

"Thank you, pet. You did so well." she praised him. He lifted his head and gave her a brilliant smile. Her heart melted, causing a mirroring smile.

"I think it's time for your reward, flip over." She said softly. He complied and they switched places, her legs now straddling his hips. She pulled down the waistband of his sweatpants, tucking them behind his sack. His cock was hard, jumping in her hand. She pumped him slowly, using his precum as lubrication. He groaned loudly, shutting his eyes. She missed his blue eyes immediately, that would not do.

"Open your eyes, pet. Watch your Miss pleasure you." she murmured, her strokes remaining even. His breaths were ragged already. He was clearly already close, but worried about disappointing her. "This is for you. Come when you like." she said gently, speeding up her efforts. She added an additional hand, circling the head with it. He began moaning in earnest, watching her stroke him. She moved one hand down to his sack, fondling gently. They quivered in her hand, soft and supple. She relished in the control she had at that moment, she could so easily squeeze and hurt him, ruin his orgasm. Clearly he enjoyed it as well, as his seed suddenly shot from the tip, covering his abdomen and her hand.

"Oh, fuck." he groaned out, hips flexing underneath her. When he finished, she quickly wiped the mess from his chest with his discarded shirt and laid on him. She listened to the steadiness of his heart beat, comforted by the rocking of his chest.

15

They fell into a routine.

She would attend to his emails at work, he would attend to his. They would come back to his apartment and she would write her little story while he continued to work. They had dinner, an orgasm and she would go home. On the weekends she would stay home and miss him, attending to her household errands.

They hadn't had sex.

Mary was delaying it, fearful of the consequences. Physically she definitely wanted to sleep with him, and was certain that he wanted it as well. She knew that he cared for her, and wanted her. If she were to complete this final act, there would be nothing he would really need her for. Mary knew a lot of things, but how to keep someone's attention was not one of them. She was accustomed to "Thank you for all the help but I'd like to get a blowjob from my neighbor now."

Okay, so that only happened once but Mary fading into the background was the usual next step.

She hoped that with George it would be different.

So far, everything with George had been different.

He was more confident, relaxed, and definitely sexually active. Mary's face flushed at the memories of how sexually active he was. After they took this next step there would be nothing left to teach, nothing for Mary to justify her position in his life.

"Would you like to stay the night?" he called out from the kitchen. Mary had one arm in her coat when she froze. She didn't answer, taking a moment to process the request. He wanted her to stay over. She would be sleeping in his bed. Next to him. He wanted to sleep with her.

"Baby?" he poked his head out into the hallway. His cheeks were fuller than she had ever seen, and the purple under his eyes was just a pastel shadow. His eyes were bright, if not a bit concerned at the moment. He looked radiant. Mary felt satisfaction at his gradual transformation. She did that.

She cleared her throat. "Why would I do that?" she asked, fastening the zipper of her jacket. He walked over and pulled her into his arms.

George inspected her face carefully. "Because that's usually how sex happens." he informed her, tone implying that was obvious.

A hit of adrenaline coursed through her. She wanted to deflower him quite desperately, but the thought of doing it now felt akin to putting her own head into a guillotine.

"You're not ready." she muttered, eyes dropping to avoid seeing his reaction.

"Pretty sure I am." he corrected, grabbing her palm and placing it on a cotton covered erection.

Mary swallowed, desperately trying to think of a way to delay the end of their arrangement.

"George, we have to do this carefully. I promised myself when we started this that I would take care of your inexperience with grace." her words came out rushed, as they usually did when she began to panic.

"What does that mean?"

"Well, you seemed so lonely and I knew you probably wouldn't get another chance."

"Whoa, hold on." he gripped her by the upper arms. "You started fooling around with me just because I was a sad lonely virgin?" His voice was high pitched and incredulous.

"Well, sort of, yes." Mary avoided his angry gaze.

"I've been a pity fuck this whole time?" he spat, letting go of her and pressing his palms over his eyes in exacerbations.

"Well, technically we haven't fu-"

"Mary!" he interrupted, eyes as cold and blue as ice. "Do you even want me?" George's voice was quiet, the pain evident in his tone.

She cleared her throat and clutched her bag tight to her breaking heart.

"You needed me, that's more important." she said, like she had to herself so often it became a psychotic mantra.

"You were wrong. I don't need you." he hissed, turning away and walking towards the living room.

Mary stepped towards the door, leaving her shattered heart on the carpet of his hallway.

"Right. Sorry for the misunderstanding." she mumbled and walked through the front door.

16

Mary crossed the street outside George's apartment. She was so numb from shock and heartbreak that she barely noticed her phone ringing as she passed by the library doors. Mary sighed, pulling out her phone and sitting on the curb.

"Excellent news, Mary." Mr. M's exuberant voice was shrill in her ear. Mary felt like there may never be true excellent news ever again.

Unless he was going to announce that a hit-man was stationed on the library roof and was about to blow her brains out.

"We are on our flight home, and I expect to see you back on that foam mat bright and early tomorrow morning." he continued, with the same forceful excitement she expected.

"Okay." she mumbled and ended the call, unable to pretend at that moment.

Mary was so tired of pretending.

Pretending to like her job, and her shitty apartment.

Pretending she wasn't hopelessly and completely in love with George.

Pretending that she didn't just ruin her chance with the only man who saw her, understood her.

She threw all of it away, and for what?

To be a good, helpful person?

No, Mary decided she wasn't a good person—she was a coward.

Mary dropped her head into her hands and wept. She didn't deserve George's forgiveness, not when she was so weak couldn't even say no to her boss.

In a moment of misery fueled delusion, Mary pulled out her phone and redialed the last number.

"Excellent news." she said, tone flat. "I quit." she hung up the call and threw the device at full velocity into the concrete outer wall of the library. It smashed into hundreds of plastic shards, satisfying some primal urge to destroy.

Now her phone felt the same way her heart did.

Now that Mary had taken care of the job she hated, the only thing she could do was get her boyfriend back.

17

"George!" Mary screamed, thumping her fists against the wood surface of his door. She didn't care how long it took, she would get him to talk to her.

"I want you." she cried, pounding loudly. "I've wanted you the whole time, since I slipped on those stupid pamphlets."

The door opened. "Was that so hard?"

George asked, voice soft and no longer angry.

"Incredibly." Mary answered, throwing herself into his arms. He caught her and stepped backwards, taking them inside.

"I'm so sorry, George." she sobbed. "I just didn't want to hurt you—" she began, interrupted when his hand covered her mouth.

"No, you didn't want to get hurt." he amended, setting her back down on the floor. Mary nodded, acknowledging that he saw through her in that regard too. "Letting someone in is difficult, if anyone knows that it's me." His chuckle was empty.

"George, I'm-" he silenced her with his lips this time, willing her to relax in his arms.

"I lied to you, too." he gasped when they parted for air. "I do need you." he leaned down and looked deep into her still watering eyes. "Will you stay?"

"You still want me to?" Mary asked, voice small but hopeful.

"Of course. You've got me hooked on this cuddling thing, I'd like to do it all night." he murmured, placing a kiss on her forehead.

His bed was large and covered with gray satin sheets. It seemed like the man just liked the color gray. She suddenly regretted complaining about the color so much.

"Not so bad is it?" he whispered into her ear. He was behind her, arms wrapped tender-ly around her waist. Over the weeks he had become an exceptionally touchy person, not that Mary was complaining.

"It's definitely much bigger than mine." she confessed, enjoying the feel of his arms. Mary moaned softly as he began nibbling the side of her neck.

"So stay." he pleaded, continuing his assault. His mouth felt so good on her neck. She was going to miss it. Sorrow creeped into Mary's chest as he continued to worship her neck with his tongue. Mary was good at many things, but hiding things was not one of them.

Gradually Mary's moans became laced with tears and turned into sobs. George detached from her neck and straightened.

"Woah, hey." he murmured, flipping her around to assess her face. "We don't have to." he cood, concluding that she was having doubts about intercourse.

"No, I want to." she blubbered, tears and snot running together on her face. She attempted to wipe them away on the sleeve of her shirt, with moderate success.

"You're crying. What did I do?" he asked, genuinely concerned he made her upset.

She laughed. He was so cute it made her cry harder.

"I just don't want this to be over." she said, George's face contorted in confusion.

"But we haven't even started yet,"

"I'm scared you won't need me anymore," she explained, her fear clear in her brown eyes. "Now you're so confident and your inbox is empty and-" she continued to blab at full velocity.

George's face relaxed in understanding.

"Oh, Mary my sweet girl." he clutched her tightly and laid on the bed, smearing her tears on his shirt. "As a beautiful woman once said to me in the library: you seem awfully worried about something that hasn't happened yet." he said, voice gentle and sweet. It made Mary cry harder.

"Did I ever say I needed your help with sex?" he asked.

Mary pondered for a moment, sniffling.

"Well, no, I guess not." Mary had assumed that experience would increase his confidence. Now that she thought about it he

never even said he wanted to be more confident. Mary's assumptions really had made
an ass out of her.

He took a deep breath. "I've really messed
this up, haven't I?" he mumbled to himself.

"No, I was-" she began to object, but was interrupted by his body weight rolling on top
of hers. He braced his arms on either side
of her head, pressing his face so close she
could feel his breath on her lips. His body
rested against hers, the weight and pressure
comforting and slightly arousing.

"I don't need you to teach me how to have
sex or manage my emails. I want those
things. I want you, sweetheart. I love it when
you order me around because I love you." he
confessed, placing a soft kiss on her trem-

bling lips. "I'm sorry I ever made you doubt that, I'll do better."

"Oh." Mary said, requiring a moment to collect herself. She had never even stopped to ponder that he began their relationship because she was inherently special to him. She had stripped him of his agency, because of her stubborn self image. Now, due to her own silly insecurities she had ruined what could have been a magical night of sexual awakening.

She had to fix this.

He cleared his throat softly. "I don't want you to feel pressured but I would like it very much if you stayed." he whispered, his words even and intentional. His length pressed against her, signaling his true intentions. Mary couldn't help but laugh. Her prince was a true gentleman.

She pushed him off and rolled him to his back. She straddled him, grinding herself on the stiff length.

"You're acting like it's my virginity and not yours." she joked, increasing the pressure on his groin. His eyebrows drew together in pleasure, eyes closing momentarily.

"To be fair you were crying." he groaned out. She undid the top of his pants, releasing his erection. It was already weeping, Mary looked down at him with satisfaction and excitement.

"If you're not crying by the time we're done, you're entitled to a refund." she teased, stroking him slowly. He groaned softly when she twisted around the head, eyes still shut in pleasure.

This would not do at all.

"Eyes up," she ordered. He opened his eyes and propped up on his shoulders, watching her stroke him. His breaths increased as she sped up, a thin layer of sweat covering his brow. His cock twitched, signaling he was near release. She released it, giving him a momentary reprieve. She slowly unbuttoned his white shirt, as she had fantasized doing for so long. His chest was damp, breaths heaving. She grabbed his cock again, resuming leisurely strokes.

She was suddenly struck with how non-traditional this situation was.

"Don't you want some more romance? I

didn't even lay out the flower petals." she asked in a teasing tone, stroking him faster.

"I'm allergic to most pollen." he gasped, shaking with the effort of holding back his orgasm.

"Good to know. You can come, baby." she whispered in his ear. He did not hesitate, letting out a series of moans and painting her hand and his abdomen in his release.

"Good boy." she said, relishing in his responding satisfied smile. His skin damp and flushed, he had never been more beautiful. Mary stripped him of his shirt and used it to wipe them both, laying next to him when she was finished.

They laid there together for some time, Mary watched him as he slowly came back from his high. She admired his ivory skin, speckled with freckles and a light dusting of hair. His softening cock resting against his abdomen, braced on either side by prominent hip bones and pointing up towards a defined waist. Mary's core was still simmering with unreleased heat, but she was content to just admire her George. This was his night after all. He rolled on to his side, facing her. His blue eyes roamed her body, pausing at her cotton shorts.

"May I?" He asked quietly, a hint of need returning to his gaze.

Mary nodded, suddenly desperate for a release of her own. He positioned himself between her thighs, carefully removing her shorts and panties. He leaned into her core and inhaled deeply. Mary moaned, the sight igniting her passion in earnest. He licked her with finesse and skill, sucking her clit as she had instructed him all those days ago. He added one finger and then two, increasing her pleasure threefold. She began climbing up to the precipice quickly, her channel quivering before she was ready.

"Stop." she instructed. George immediately paused and withdrew his fingers, placing them in his mouth. Mary closed her eyes for a moment, soon he would be able to make her orgasm without even touching her.

"Now." she said, unable to elaborate while her whole body burned for him. He nodded in understanding, removing his pants and placing himself between her legs. He was already erect again, aroused by pleasing her. Her heart burned in conjunction with her body. Mary could have taken control and walked him through it, but in that moment she didn't need to. She knew George and George knew her body. He needed to do this, to prove to himself more than her that he could do this well, that he could please her. Slowly he pressed himself against her entrance, hand trembling slightly. She propped up on her elbow, putting him within reaching distance. Mary grasped his neck and waist, hoping the contact would strengthen him.

"That's it, baby." she cooed in his ear. "Make love to me." she ordered gently, placing her forehead against his. He thrust in with one smooth movement, her slickness easing him. Mary could not stifle the loud moan that poured from her mouth at the feeling of being filled by him at last. He silenced her with his mouth, the force of his kiss pushing her flat on her back. He thrust again, with his cock and tongue, sending jolts of pleasure to her womb.

"Oh fuck," she groaned. "It's perfect, you're perfect."

His thrusts were steady and rhythmic, rubbing against her inside walls in just the right place. She needed more.

"For you," he panted. "It's for you." He buried his head into the crook of her neck, concentrating on his goal. She took one of his hands and placed it on her clit, rubbing his finger against her quickly in the motion she needed.

His head snapped up, eyes locking with hers. "Can you?"

"You can." she reassured, panting between words. She was already hovering on the precipice from his skillfully foreplay and magnificent cock, she only required a final push. His eyes blazed as he pressed her clit and thrust rhythmically, determined to push them over the edge together. It was unbelievably sexy and hurled Mary into the most intense orgasm of her life. Mary threw her head back and screamed, her inner walls contracting around him. George let out a groan of his own and thrust into her in abandon, claiming his own release.

"Why weren't you mad when I came back?"

she asked when they had recovered, lay-ing next to each other on the now rumpled sheets. She thought it was bizarre he had gotten over her dishonesty so quickly.

"I watched you smash your phone from my window, I felt like that was punishment enough." he explained, causing Mary to roll her eyes. "I also can't pretend that I don't worship the ground you walk on." he placed a soft kiss on her temple.

"Plus," he added, "I really was a sad, lonely virgin." he joked, grunting as he stretched.

Mary laughed, elbowing his slim abdomen. "And yet I fell in love with you anyway."

"I know." he smiled. " I thought you could tell too, clearly I was wrong." he admitted with a chuckle.

"Have you ever thought about programming a mind reading device? Would prevent a lot of misunderstandings." she teased.

"I never said I was a good programmer."

18
One month later...

"*I can't do it, I won't.*" *The Prince mumbled into her bosom, hiding away from his problems. Mistress sighed and continued to stroke his hair.*

Their time was over.

The Prince's wedding was scheduled in the morning, and he was embracing his mistress, tucked into the safe confines of her arms and bed.

"You must." she said calmly. Mistress had grieved their eventual separation for several months, now resigned to loving her Prince from afar.

"Must I? I have brothers." he replied. Mistress snorted, the Prince's brothers were just as spoiled as him but were significantly deficient in both intellect and compassion.

"You were born for this," she said.

"I was also born to love you." he confessed, sighing sadly.

He lifted his head out of her cleavage to stare into her reassuring eyes.

"How could I ever rule a kingdom when my queen is not beside me?" he pleaded, his voice *full of anguish. She gently gripped his chin, bringing his handsome face closer.*

"The same as many kings before you." she cooed, placing a sweet kiss on his lips. "I do not need a title or a crown. When you look at me I feel as if I am your entire kingdom."

He groaned and rolled away from her, his bare chest facing the worn wood of the ceiling. He was a magnificent sight, pants drifting low on his hips, revealing the top curls of his pubic hair. Mistress had the sudden urge to run her fingers through it and tug.

"How can I be a husband to another woman when every part of me belongs to you." he called out, reaching out for answers from his deity.

"Most royal marriages are not love matches." she said, rolling towards him and placing her

cheek on his chest, running a palm through the patch of hair below his navel.

"I would be expected to produce an heir." he said, despair ringing clear in his voice. The words morphed into knives of pain lodged in Mistress' gut. "My cock cannot even stand without your command!" he admitted, pointing towards the subject of discussion.

"Really?" she asked in surprise, amusement dancing in her eyes. He nodded meekly, flushed with embarrassment. Looking down at the groin of his tailored trousers, Mistress' had the sudden need to test his statement.

"I tried to pleasure myself, to prove that I could perform when the time came." he explained, pulling out the soft member to demonstrate. "And yet, he laid there. Useless and slumbering, *offended I would even attempt such a thing." he explained, gripping his sleeping cock and shifting it side to side. Just as he had predicted, he didn't even twitch.*

Mistress giggled, surprised how much his cock's loyalty made her heart sing. "He just needs a little motivation." Mistress teased, removing her thin undergarment. The Prince's eyes roved her body, hunger clear in them. Alas, his cock remained flaccid, waiting for command. Mistress was impressed. As much fun as this exploration was, admiring her Prince's goods had made her too needy.

Mistress straddled his abdomen, smearing her juices on the hard ridges of his muscles. The Prince moaned softly and placed his hands on her hips to aid her grinding.

"He better wake up, or his Mistress will be very disappointed." she threatened, pushing her clit against him. The pressure was delicious, but Mistress needed more.

The Prince pushed her pelvis down onto his already throbbing erection. Mistress was elated, rubbing herself up and down the length of him.

"Oh, good boy." she praised with a brilliant smile. She slipped him inside and sat, burying him to the hilt. The Prince let out a loud groan.

"I'm afraid I won't last," he admitted, pistoning his hips roughly. He was so deep the thrusts settled in Mistress' chest cavity, urging her to climax.

"Yes, give me your come." she demanded, leaning forward and wrapping her hand around his throat. His life was physically in her hand, just

like hers had been in his for years. His thrusts were feral, hitting her most pleasurable ridges. She came with a series of moans, drowning out his own sounds of release.

Eventually she dismounted and lay beside him, admiring his sated form. Mistress didn't know what would happen tomorrow, and ultimately it was not up to her.

It was the Prince's choice.

"I trust you." she said, placing a palm over his heart.

"I will not disappoint you." he replied, placing a kiss on the back of her hand.

George was sitting on the couch. His long fingers turned the page of the notebook, the red polished tips skirting across the paper. His gaze focused on the words of the page, delicate brows furrowed. His hair was messy, a stray section hanging in his line of vision. He paid it no attention, engrossed in the story. Her prince was truly beautiful. Mary continued to admire him, acutely aware of his movements. She did not miss when his breathing sped slightly, and she definitely did not miss his hand trailing up and wrapping around the side of his neck. His palm pressed to the underside of his jaw, thumb gently pressing into his Adam's apple. He let out a few shuddering breaths, a flush beginning to creep up his chest. Mary felt a twinge of heat to her sex.

"You want me to choke you." she observed. It wasn't a question because it didn't need to be.

He startled out of his fantasy, snapped his gaze to hers and lowered his hand back down to the couch. He didn't reply but the flush on his cheeks was enough confirmation. He tilted his head to the side, exposing his pale neck for her. She could see the subtle movements of his heartbeat beneath the skin, her mouth was suddenly filled with saliva.

She seated herself on his lap, removed the notebook from his grasp and placed it on the cushion to his side. Miss grabbed the hair at the nape of his neck and tilted his head backwards, causing his lips to part in surprised pleasure. Her nose and lips skirted up the side of his neck, finishing centimeters from his ear.

"It makes me wonder: Why do you want that?" she whispered in a contemplative tone. The back of his neck was slick against her forearm. Was he aroused or ashamed? She shifted her pelvis slightly. The hardness beneath her core made itself known.

"Did it make you hard, pet?" she teased, continuing to grind against him. He let out a small groan.

"Use your voice." she instructed.

"Yes, Miss." he moaned, his voice small and shaky.

"Why is that, pet? Do you wish to experience the pleasure of breath play?" she asked, tugging again on his hair. She placed a kiss just under his ear and shifted her hips once more.

He let out a louder moan.

"N-No, Miss." he answered, bucking upwards against her. The thin barrier of his pants did not dampen the shocks of pleasure caused by his bucking.

"Perhaps it is because I own you. Your lips, your hands, your cock, and even your breath." she mused, nipping at his ear lobe. She was rewarded with a soft whimper. She straightened her back, bringing her hand to join the other clasped at his nape. She adjusted the placement of her hands. Her palms were wrapped around the sides of his neck, fingers interlaced at the back. She pressed her thumbs gently on either side of his trachea.

"Don't look away." she instructed. His pleading gaze fixed to hers, begging for her touch, her pleasure. She leaned forward, their lips almost touching.

Carefully she increased the pressure of her thumbs, ensuring that his breathing remained steady. Her hands were a cage around his most vital area, offering a brace of support but capable of great harm. She watched as the color of his face deepened and the focus of his eyes wavered. She released the pressure of her hands, and waited for the gasp of his breath. He returned to her quickly, his cock twitching beneath her. She kissed him roughly, needing the reassurance of his breaths in her mouth. He mirrored her desperation, coaxing her tongue to dance with his.

"Please, Miss. May I touch you?" he pleaded. Her core pulsed in response, her respiration rate increasing.

"Yes, Pet." she answered, desperate for the feel of his touch. She crashed their lips together again and buried her hands in his hair, wishing to inhale his essence into her lungs. His arms did not hesitate to wrap around her back, pressing her breasts to his chest. He could feel her rapid breaths against him, which spurred his sharp thrusts against her. His hands traveled down to the globes of her ass, guiding her hips in their grinding.

"Did you like it?" she breathed, yanking his head back to look at her.

" Yes." he confirmed. His eyes were steady but pleading.

"Why?" she asked, increasing the pressure of her hips against his. She purposely rubbed her pussy against the length of his shaft, noting the dampness left in her wake.

"B-because I'm yours." he stuttered.

"Keep going." she ordered. Her lips began to kiss and nip at his neck.

"Because you take such good care of me. You-you know what I need, and give me what I deserve." he panted. He struggled to finish the sentence due to the pleasure of her ministrations.

"And what do you deserve right now?" she asked, nipping his neck harder. He shuttered beneath her.

"To make you come. Please, Miss. Please let me make you feel good." he pleaded. His bucking underneath her was wild, his skin damp with the effort of restraint.

"Hmm, I don't think so." she responded, his breath caught for a moment. "But I am in the mood for an orgasm. So you are going to stay very still while I use my cock to get off. Eyes open. If you come without permission there will be consequences." she said. She stood and removed her damp panties.

"Open," she instructed. His mouth opened without hesitation, and she placed the ball of cloth inside. His jaw strained but his gaze remained steadfast on her. Mary knew how much he loved this particular move.

"Good boy." she smiled.

She straddled his lap once more after extracting his erection from his pants. It was weeping at the tip, begging for her attention. She felt sorry for the poor appendage, since she had no plans of doing so. A quick stroke of her hand was rewarded with a tortured groan from her prince, his head thrown back. She removed his shirt, admiring the sleek contours of his chest. She gently stroked the light smattering of chest hair, noting that his torso was also damp with sweat. Her poor pet was suffering for her. A new rush of need filled her womb.

She pushed on his shoulders, leaning him back into the corner of the sectional. He placed his hands on her hips gently in support. She began to rub her pussy along the length of him, the notch of his head rubbing tenderly against her clit. The head of his cock continued to weep with every swipe of her core. He continued to moan with every pass, muffled by the cotton still stuffed in his mouth. Saliva ran down his chin, the vision causing Mary to speed up her efforts. She braced her arms on the couch above his head, increasing the pace of her work further. Suddenly she needed his eyes, needed his words. Mary ripped the panties from his mouth and tossed them across the room. He lifted his gaze to hers in alarm.

"Talk to me, pet. Make your Miss come." she

demanded, her breath shaky.

"I-I don't know if I can, Miss." he breathed. "I'm trying so hard n-not to come." he continued, the strain on his face evident.

"Your pussy is too hot and wet on me, and your tits are so close to my mouth. I'm drooling for you." he panted, residue of saliva still on his face. Miss brought her face up to his and gave the trail of spit a long lick, swallowing it down.

"Oh fuck, oh Jesus." he swore, shutting his eyes for a moment to collect himself. Miss immediately stilled her movements. His eyes snapped open.

"Oh, no, no. Please don't stop. I'm sorry, I won't look away." he promised. Miss continued her grinding, although at a slower pace.

She ground her clit against the bulbous head of his cock, causing several droplets of liquid to escape.

"My cock is drooling for you." he whimpered. "It needs your come. It's begging for it. I'm begging for it. Please, miss. Please." he begged. She could feel his balls tightening under her ass. Her poor pet was trying so hard.

"You have been such a good boy. You've earned to come with your master. Would you like that?" she asked, tightening the movements of her clit.

"If it pleases you." he panted, barely able to push out the words. His whole body was shuddering, desperate for release. Still, his need to please his master was stronger.

Tears began to fill his eyes, his torment and conviction at war within them. The friction compounded with his submission was too much for Mary to bear. Lightning bolts of pleasure crawled up her body, fueling the contractions of her pussy. The sensation of her slick heat and pulsations was too much for her George to bear.

"Oh fuck, oh fuck." he yelled out. He came with such force that the spurts of his release covered his abdomen and chest.

Mary placed a soft kiss to his mouth, luxuriating in the softness of his lips and his devotion.

"You are such a good, good boy." she whispered, and she meant every word.

Some time later Mary was laying on his

chest, enjoying the feel of his skin as he finished reading the latest entry in her notebook.

"How do they end up together?" he asked, placing the notebook down once he finished. "Does he abdicate? Do they stay together in secret?"

Mary took a deep breath and hummed in pleasure. Her post orgasm lethargy still lingered in her bones and tongue.

"I don't think it matters." she replied honestly. She looked up into her prince's eyes, they were gazing down at her with adoration and devotion. "They love each other, they'll figure it out."

To my family, for humoring my bizarre cat-related questions.

To Luke, my cat, for being a handsome prince.

To Molly, as always, for everything.

1

Prince Meets Witch

*T*he swamp was dark and foul.

The Prince was not used to unpleasant smells, his royal nose scrunched as he waded through the brown putrid water. It would likely take a week to scrub off the disgusting residue from his expensive leather boots. His Mistress would take care of it, she always took care of his needs and made sure he lived in the lap of luxury. Her supple curves and commanding voice flitted through his mind. The warmth in his chest fueled him as he trekked through the bog, validated in his journey. He would not think of the sludge in his socks, he would definitely stop gagging.

The small shack came into view quickly, thank the Lord above. The Prince rapped four times on the aged wooden door, heart hammering in his throat. The Witch answered the door, smaller than he expected. She was not old, and not particularly ugly. She also was not happy, which he did expect.

"I've paid my taxes," she said, crossing her arms

over her chest.

"Good to hear, may I come in?" he replied, impatience clear in his voice. Her eyes remained suspicious as she held the door open in reluctant invitation.

She led him to a small dining table with two rickety chairs, motioning for him to sit.

"I won't take up much of your time." he vowed, mostly because the smell of the swamp was making him nauseated. "I need your help."

Her eyebrows raised. "And why should I help you?" she asked through narrowed eyes. He couldn't blame her for being distrustful of him; the crown generally wasn't kind to outcasts.

"Don't you have pity for a man in love?" he asked, letting every drop of his misery pour out *onto his face. He was to be married to a woman he didn't love, while his Mistress suffered.*

"No." the Witch said, joining him at the bargaining table. Men in love were pathetic and held no space in her heart.

He cleared his throat, now determined.

"What do you want?" he said. "Money, land, title?" he asked, tone increasing in desperation.

Her laugh was sharp and very cackle-like. This was not the first time a royal sibling had offered her items of status, she was no more interested this time. The Witch was not an evil woman, though perhaps slightly bitter at the circumstances she had found herself in.

"I don't know if I can help you." he said with amusement in her eyes. "What do you need?"

"My Mistress." he began, eyes filling with love at the thought of her. "I cannot fulfill my obligations as a prince because I need her as a man." he explained.

The Witch's eyes softened. This particular predicament was too close to her heart to ignore. She did have pity for this Prince in love, she could see he was desperate in his need for his Mistress, but she didn't yet understand why he needed her help.

"Why not give up your title?" she asked, doubting his ability to sacrifice.

"I know nothing else. I was bred and raised to be a prince. How could I support her in a village when I have no skills? Besides, she won't allow me." He stood and began pacing. "She's insistent that my obligation to the Kingdom is more

important than my obligation to love her!" he shouted, gesticulating wildly with his hands.

The Witch giggled, her respect for this Mistress was growing. She knew what it was like to swallow one's own desire for the good of others. The image of long golden hair and a shy smile churned her gut. She also knew how quickly resentment could build and carve away one's heart.

She walked over to the small fireplace, stopping in front of the selection of herbs. The Prince did not yet understand what it was like to lose it all, to truly struggle. He did not appreciate the hard work it took to earn true love. His Mistress also did not know the vulnerability required. They were both stranded, joined in an equally distorted love.

Suddenly it became clear how the Witch could help him. She placed the herbs in the pot of boiling water, infusing intentions into the mixture as she stirred. It had been many years since she had done it, and never purposefully. Love fueled her, just as it did the Prince.

"What will you do to become worthy?" the Witch said, pouring a serving of the brew into a ceramic mug.

"Anything. Everything." he promised, honesty shining in his eyes. She held out the mug in front of him. He took it without hesitation and sipped.

There was a puff of smoke and all that remained in his place was a pile of clothes. The Witch crouched down, worried for a moment she made an error in her recipe. To her relief there was rustling beneath the fabric and a handsome black cat emerged. The Witch let out a relieved breath and grabbed the necklace that pooled around him. She adjusted the fit, fastening it around his neck as a makeshift collar.

She lifted him into her arms and carried the small furry Prince to the front steps of her home. She carefully set him down.

"Good luck, Prince." She bid him farewell and closed the wooden door with a soft click.

2

Mary Meets
Python

Mary put down her pen and looked up at her man.

George was in the kitchen, adjusting his tie using the reflection from the hallway mirror. He still looked princely in her opinion, even more handsome now that she knew how kind and considerate he was. Her initial fascination was purely aesthetic, but over the months they had spent together she had grown to appreciate the intensity and bluntness of his love. Unlike the Prince in her notebook, George didn't have to seek any help in order to be worthy. He already had everything figured out it seemed. He didn't have to panic about feeling adequate enough to meet her family.

"Remind me again why we have to do this?" Mary flopped back onto the couch and stretched, moaning at the pleasure of easing her stiff muscles.

"Because we are in love, which means you have to meet my parents." he explained, slipping his gangly arms through a dark gray blazer. Mary hummed in appreciation as she admired him. He had allowed her to make adjustments to his wardrobe, a small amount of color added to his rotation. He still dressed like a used car salesman, but one that was not allergic to happiness. Mary imagined he was selling her at an auction, listing her admirable attributes in front of a room full of hungry men. He would be stuttering, unable to look away from her.

She groaned lightly and rolled off the couch, standing to join him at the mirror. He pulled her into his arms, back to his front. The matching gray dress she wore clung to her round silhouette, now framed with his long pale fingers on her waist.

"Plus," he mumbled, lips pressed to her

neck. "I reward good behavior handsome-ly."

Mary rolled her eyes, but her core heated. As her submissive, he would be doing no such thing. She would be handing out the rewards, or punishments. The idea of his capitulation to her depravity did fuel her bravery. She had never met any previous partner's parents before, and she felt self-conscious about the whole affair. She didn't have much accomplishment to brag about, currently working as George's executive assistant since impulsively quitting her part time job. Mary never regretted it for a second– she enjoyed spending every possible moment with her boyfriend. She knew that his parents worked in finance and kept to themselves but that was all.

What did they expect for George?

Would she be good enough?

Mary took a deep breath and put on her armor of optimism. She loved him and that was enough. She had to be brave and take care of George.

"Let's just get it over with," she said, throwing her purse around her shoulder. The cartoon cats that littered the front of it had brought her joy. She bought it at a flea market after one of the toddlers at her previous work slimed in its predecessor. Now the bright colors and animated whiskers made her question herself.

Was it too immature?

Was she too immature?

What did it say about her character that she would parade around in public with a bag that was probably made for children?

The feline portraits gazed at her while they drove to their destination, the hum of the Prius too quiet to drown out their mocking whiskered faces. She had just resigned to toss the damn purse out the car window when they pulled up to a gate.

A goddamn wrought iron gate with an intercom.

"George," Mary said warily. "You never said your parents were rich." Her heart began to hammer in panic, she was not expecting this. Mary had never been to any house that had a gate. Most of the places she lived didn't even have a functioning fence. Her last apartment only had resident possum to guard it. The fella had a gnarled face and was uncommonly large, which was really all he needed to dissuade anyone from entering the property. He was a sweety, Mary remembered. Most nocturnal mammals get a bad rap, she identified with their misunderstood nature. Regardless, Mary was grateful when George asked her to move in a few months ago. She spent all her time there anyways, there was no point in paying rent for no reason.

"They're comfortable." he replied, the gate opening for him. That was rich people speak. Mary now deeply regretted not throwing her car purse out the window when she had a chance. She could always conveniently leave it in the car. Where would she put her phone? Her breasts were generous but not large enough to hide a smartphone. Panic heated her skin, inevitably causing her skin to flush. She would be meeting his parents, sweaty and red, a tomato girlfriend. The look of concerns on his face snapped her out of the internal ramble.

"George, you should know I've never ridden a horse or played golf." she said, panic squeezing her throat. She would certainly be squeezing his throat for this later. The memory of choking her love distracted her for a moment before the view of the mansion plunked her back to reality.

He chuckled and grabbed her hand.

"You're good enough for me, don't worry about them." he tried to reassure her. Mary was very worried about them. They would take one look at her, and see that she was common scum. A cheap beefsteak tomato in a garden of heirlooms. They would know that she was unworthy of their son and spit on her face.

Probably.

Mary didn't actually know what rich people did when they were mad. Or what they did at all, really.

She took a deep breath and squeezed his sweaty palm. He was nervous too. She gazed into his blue eyes, they were filled with soft reassurance. She needed to be brave for him, he needed her. Mary shook her head, remembering the night she deflowered him. She was worried that her value to him was directly tied to service she could provide. It was a horrible assumption on her part which happened to be her worst character flaw. She constantly had to remind herself that he wanted her. He chose her, socioeconomic status be damned. She took several deep breaths, focusing on the lovely man next to her. He had never brought a girl home before, and he deserved a good experience. Her insecurities could wait.

The mansion was surrounded by a neatly manicured lawn and garden. Mary was sure there must be a landscaper involved. One of her aunts married a landscaper. He was from Columbia and had a habit of wearing speedos to family beach functions. Mary shuddered at the memory.

A tall, slim couple was waiting for them at the entrance of the estate, pleasant smiles on their faces. Mary felt clunky as they walked from the car, the modest two inch heel she wore felt like stilts. She should have worn Spanx with this dress, people with his amount of money had personal train-ers. Home gyms too, probably. Mary meant to start going to the gym but then kept re-membering that she hated exercise. Besides, she was usually on top during intercourse, which should count as cardio.

"Mom, Dad," George greeted, giving them each a hug and polite kiss on the cheek. This was good. They had a good relationship. Mary's chest unclenched slightly. "This is Mary." He motioned to his love, pride in his eyes.

"It's nice to meet you, Mrs-" Mary began, unable to finish as she was pulled into a brutal hug. George's mother was a python, her arms were deceptively strong for how slender they were. She smelled good, like a perfume Mary could never afford.

"Wendy, but mom is fine." she said, still squeezing the life out of the young woman. Okay, Mrs Python was welcoming at least. "This is Richard." she introduced, finally letting Mary go. She hoped that George's father wasn't also a hugger because she did not have the breath holding skills to survive. Luckily he simply shook her hand and smiled. George must take after him.

They were a handsome couple in the way that a life of privilege allowed. Both had

dark hair and blue eyes, natural creases surrounded their eyes and lips.

"Shall we?" George grabbed Mary's hand
and led her into the home. Mrs. Python started spouting off factoids about the property, which gave Mary time to quiet her racing heart. The home had five bedrooms and
six bathrooms which was puzzling but Mary
felt it impolite to inquire. Mary remembered
that when she had two cats it was recom-
mended to have three litter boxes. Rich people must also need extra choices to defecate
into. They hired a gardener but Richard did
all the cooking. George really must take after his dad. Mary could seldom count in one
hand how often he let her cook. Her job in
the kitchen was to keep him company and
act as the dessert most days. It was a good

deal Mary could not refuse.

Finally they reached the dining room which was well decorated and sported a large oak table. Suddenly a loud yelp and the sound of skin slapping cascaded down the hall, heading straight for Mary. Something wet and fleshy hit her shins.

Some would call it a dog, but it was essentially a mobile bag of wrinkles and slobber.

"Stewart!" Mrs Python exclaimed, cheeks flushed with embarrassment. Mary laughed and kneeled to pet the dog, her fingers sinking into the crevices between furry folds. It was absolutely disgusting and she loved him already. The folds weighed down the skin beneath his eyes making him look both old and tired.

"It's okay, I love old ugly dogs." she reassured, continuing to caress the canine's unpleasant fur.

"Well, you did fall in love with me." George joked, giving the dog in question a firm head pat. The puppy waddled away as suddenly as he appeared, leaving a trail of slime behind him.

Absolutely foul.

Mary's chest felt light, all of her worries gone for the moment. The little guy didn't know how ugly he was, and he didn't care. He was stronger than her, in that regard.

"Well, I'm starving. Shall we eat?" Richard said, rubbing his flat abdomen.

George and his father disappeared to the

kitchen in search of the food, Mary and the python naturally began setting the table. Luckily there was only one fork and knife set for each person, clearly they were not complicated rich people.

Dinner was pleasant.

The meal was simple and delicious, nothing deconstructed or in the form of a savory foam. Mary kept the conversation trained on George, curious to know more about the man that had quickly taken over her heart and life.

"Oh, he did everything," Mrs Python said, pride glittering in her eyes. "Violin, Piano, Chess, I think there was even a math club at one point." she gushed, dinner completely forgotten. Mary was shocked that George could play so many instruments, he had never mentioned it before. Piano made sense, his fingers were certainly long enough. Why didn't he have a piano in his apartment? It might be a space issue but Mary was pretty sure they could find room for an electric keyboard. This seemed like a voluntary omission. She would have to ask him about it.

"I only went to one meeting." George clarified meekly, swallowing a bite of green beans. "Turns out you have to talk to people to be in a club."

Mary's heart deflated. She didn't like to remember how much her love struggled to connect as a child. The George she knew was so goofy and open, it was a shame no one ever got to see that until now. Some sick twisted part of her enjoyed that this new happy George belonged only to her.

"Were you in any clubs?" Richard asked, turning the conversation to Mary. Her breath stalled for a moment. How could she share without revealing her inadequacy? Mary did not play any instruments due to the cost of rental. When the teacher passed her the pamphlet that listed the prices, she threw it straight into the trash bin. No point even getting her hopes up. Her mother always made comments about how they couldn't afford vacations, there was no way they could spend hundreds of dollars on a trumpet. Mary didn't play sports because she had exertional asthma and two left feet. Where did that expression come from anyway? Was anyone actually born with two left feet? Why not two right feet?

George's parents looked at her with expectation, like perhaps she should answer their question. Mary flushed.

"Oh, I didn't have a lot of time after school. Too busy studying." It wasn't an outright lie, Mary was very diligent about completing her homework to maintain good grades. Her mother always said how important a good education was. She wouldn't be able to take care of them on minimum wage forever. Unfortunately, that lesson didn't stick since she was working for minimum wage until a few months ago. She briefly considered going to college but didn't want to waste so much money if she wasn't 100% sure. What if she wasn't as smart as she thought she was? If she had to drop out she would be left with thousands of dollars of student loan debt with no job prospects. She would be stuck moving from trailer park to trailer park like her mother. Mary shuttered internally. She was acutely aware of George's eyes on her, slightly narrowed in suspicion. They would need to talk about this later.

George stood, holding his hand out to his love. "Shall I show you the second floor?" he asked, rhetorically. Mary began to object, offering to do the dishes first. The older couple adamantly refused and pushed them toward the staircase. Mary laughed, George really did take after his parents.

George led her upstairs, a trail of photos lining the wall of the hallway. George's whole life was chronicled in those pictures. Floppy haired toddler to cap and gowned graduate. In every single photo, his parents were by his side. Mary's heart panged in envy, jealous that he had his parents unwavering support. Mary's parents had good intentions, that she was sure of. They just always had something else to do, somewhere else to be. Maybe Mary just never did anything worth showing up for.

Mary was disappointed that George's childhood bed did not have star wars bed sheets. It was gray, the thread count no doubtedly about a million. Mary flopped down onto the comforter, thread count confirmed against her back. She exhaled loudly, attempting to release the tension in her chest. George watched her, quietly flicking the lock on the door handle. He stepped towards her, dropping to his knees at her feet. She propped up onto her elbows watching him with a heated gaze. He carefully removed her heels, placing them to the side gently. George planted a trail of soft kisses up her leg starting at the inside of her ankle. Mary let out a soft moan.

"George, this isn't a good idea." she breathed, his lips crawling up her thigh.

"I've never brought a girl in here." he said, hot breath causing moisture to pool at her core. "and you seem a little tense." He hiked her dress up to reveal the lace panties that covered her. She had expanded her panty collection when it became apparent how much he enjoyed them. "Plus, they're probably hoping a put a grandbaby in you."

Mary didn't have any mental space to argue when his mouth made contact with her pussy.

"Why did you lie?" he asked, voice muffled. Mary moaned at the vibration of his voice against her most sensitive place.

"What, I didn't-" she began, squeaking when he pinched her clit between his teeth. The sharp pain was quickly replaced with extreme pleasure. She didn't even know she liked that. George had become more bold as their relationship progressed, sometimes 'topping from the bottom'. Mary didn't usually mind. If Mary was honest with herself, sometimes she needed it.

"Try again." he scolded, increasing the pace

of his tongue against her.

"I didn't want to disappoint them," she panted, "disappoint you." She moaned at the building pleasure, the summit of her orgasm was within reaching distance.

His mouth was suddenly gone and Mary was about to cry about it.

"The only way you could disappoint me is by not being true to yourself," he quoted her from all those months ago, his blue eyes shone with love and sadness. "You are my entire universe, and if that is shameful what does that say of me?" he whispered against her inner thigh. He didn't like her self doubt. Mary couldn't help but reach for him. She grabbed his face and pulled it up towards hers. The kiss was deep and sensual, filled with love and longing.

"I'm sorry," she breathed against his lips. To degrade her worth was to degrade his love. Mary never wanted George to feel anything but whole and happy.

Suddenly two long fingers pierced her. Mary moaned, a little too loudly for the context. The context being his parents existing just down stairs. The possibility of being caught was arousing. Mary never considered herself an exhibitionist. She would have to give George a blowjob in the car later to test that out. She pressed her mouth to her lover's shoulder in an attempt to muffle her pleasure.

"If you do not see your worth, then I need to work harder." he panted against her neck, working his tongue against it. His fingers hooked and caressed her inner channel in the exact way he knew drove her crazy.

"Make me come." she ordered.

"Yes, Sweetheart." he grunted. Mary's toes curled at the modification of her honorific. She was not a Mistress, that title was too distant for the love they shared. She was his Sweetheart, his literal ball and chain. It was something he could call her at the grocery store and no one would be none the wiser. But they would know.

When his thumb pressed against her clit, she was gone. Thrown over the edge of climax, pleasure radiated down her limbs in a firestorm.

George softly brought her down with gentle

touches and whispered sweet murmurs.

He softly righted her panties and slipped her shoes back on, planting one last soft kiss on her lace clad mound. Mary did not offer to reciprocate, she knew that George enjoyed denial. It made his next orgasm even stronger. However she would not let this encounter be only about her.

"Why don't you play piano anymore?" she asked, his mouth froze against her skin. George did not answer, just started nuzzling his nose against her mons in an attempt to distract her. He didn't want to talk about this. Mary's chest burned, she needed to get it out of him.

"George..." Mary warned, resisting the desire that began to rise once again. "I believe

I asked you a question." her tone was stern, this was not a game he could win.

He sighed and stood, moving to sit next to her on the bed.

"When I was senior there was this big recital," he began, eyes trained on the floor. "It was a big deal, there were several scouts from the conservatory," He laid back and threw his arm over his eyes. "And I flubbed it, just froze, didn't play one goddamn note." His voice was tense, clearly this story was hard to repeat.

"I never played piano again after that." he finished, taking a deep breath.

Mary leaned over and straddled him, removing his arm from his face. His blue eyes were vulnerable, begging her not to talk about this anymore.

It was too bad Mary loved his begging.

"George, that was twenty years ago." she pointed out. Clearly if he got to the level of conservatory he was good and liked it to some degree. Mary didn't understand why he would avoid a hobby for so long from one case of stage fright. She placed a chaste kiss on his lips.

"Can we come back to this later?" he asked, tone anguished. She loved this man too much to let him suffer too intensely. Best to save the suffering for when he was naked.

"Okay," she agreed, and dismounted him.

"Shall we go have some dessert?" he asked.

Mary giggled. "I think you already did."

3
Mistress Meets Cat

*T*he castle was in a panic, which matched
the Mistress' worried heart.

*The Prince had been missing for several days,
vanishing the morning of his wedding. She was
not completely surprised he had disappeared,
she could sense his distress at the proposed mar-*

riage. It had broken her heart a million times, the thought of her Prince belonging to someone else. She fantasized many times about running away with him. They could raise cattle or grow potatoes. The idea of the Prince wearing cotton or going anywhere near dirt was laughable. He deserved better than the peasant life she could give him. She had missed him terribly but more importantly she was worried for his safety. Where could he have gone?

There was a meow outside the door to her bedroom. The Mistress' brows furrowed in confusion. The barn cats did not usually wander into the castle and they most definitely didn't meow.

She carefully opened the door a crack, gazing through the gap at her feline visitor.

The cat was large and handsome, most definite-

ly male. His eyes were a piercing, very familiar blue. His fur was absolutely filthy and Mistress kneeled down to inspect his glittering collar. Her stomach dropped when she recognized the necklace that hung around his neck. Why would the Prince give his necklace to a cat? Unless...

The Mistress walked over to the vanity and sat facing the door.

"Come here," she commanded. The cat ran to her and leaped onto the table, causing her to startle in surprise. Cats were not known to be obedient. "If you are the Prince, give me two short meows." The cat complied. Mistress collapsed on the table, letting out a tortured groan.

"Oh Prince, what have you done?"

4
Punishment

A muffled groan caused Mary to pause her writing. She smiled and looked up at her pet. He was tied to the headboard and gagged, cock hard and straining.

"Is there a problem?" she asked, feigning disinterest. A desperate moan replied to her, lighting up desire in her core. She placed the notebook on the desk in the corner of the bedroom, and crawled up the bed towards her bound love. His skin was flushed and breaths were rapid, cock weeping for her. It was truly a beautiful sight. She removed the cloth from his mouth and tied it around his eyes, blinding him.

She left him there for a moment, padding to the kitchen to grab the supplies. When she returned he was still desperate, if not more from the heightened arousal of the blindfold.

She carefully took an ice cube from the bowl and trailed it from the center of his chest down to his bellybutton. He hissed, breaths stuttering from the cold.

"Surprised?" she asked. "It can be uncomfortable, being surprised."

He answered in a tortured groan.

She continued to trace the lines of his abdomen with the cold cube, arousal growing at his building desperation.

"It can also be intensely pleasurable." she breathed against the head of his cock.

Without another word she swallowed his cock, tossing the ice cube away. His need was making her impatient. She lowered her mouth all the way to his base, core heating with his escalating moans.

"Oh fuck, baby. Please, sweetheart." he begged, barely able to speak.

She lifted her mouth off him for a breath.

"Please, what?" she asked.

His body was shuttering.

"Please let me come." he pleaded, his desperation was delicious.

"Why should I?" she asked, her mouth hovered millimeters over his head.

"I'll do anything," he grunted, barely able to speak.

"Deal." she murmured, taking him all the way and squeezing his sack in the way he needed. He shouted his release, hot jets of seed hitting the back of her throat.

"Thank you." he breathed.

Mary unbound him, settling into her home on his chest.

They lay together, George's body relaxed and sated. He was so beautiful, so perfect for her. Was she perfect for him? Mary's mind was still tumbling, playing back all the choices she made in the meeting with his parents. Should she have brought a gift? Wine? Mary didn't like wine so she wouldn't even know where to start. Would they like expensive wine or artisanal? Mary's aunt made moonshine once, but the older couple didn't seem like bathtub moonshine people.

George leaned his head down and sniffed dramatically in her ear, causing Mary to laugh.

"What are you doing?" she giggled.

"I think I smell smoke coming out of there." he joked. "What's going on in that delicious head of yours?" he asked, placing a kiss on her forehead.

Mary sighed and buried her face into his firm chest. It was embarrassing how much thought she was giving one meeting with his parents.

"Have I done something to make you feel bad?" he asked, blaming himself for her pre-occupation. "Do you need more oral? Because that's not a probl-"

Mary shook her head, interrupting his blab-bering.

"I just want them to like me." she said hon-estly, unable to lie to her George. "I don't want them to think that you could do bet-ter." she trailed her hand from the patch of hair on his pale chest down to his bellybutton. Touching George was so much easier than talking about her insecurities. He had a pretty impressive refractory period for someone his age. Last week after he came she ordered him to keep going and he did. She didn't even know men could come twice without stopping. It was probably his extended virgin hood; all of his spermies were just pent up in there.

"Baby." George began, interrupting her train of thought. "Why is it so hard to believe that they like you?" he asked. Mary really would prefer not to talk about this anymore, there were much more pleasurable things that she could be doing.

"Why would they? I haven't done anything to show them that they should." Mary explained, her tone implied that this was obvious. Her hand followed the trail downwards from his navel, landing on his semi-erect cock.

"I see." he nodded. Suddenly he rolled away from her and pulled on his boxer briefs.

"I'm cutting you off." he said sternly, hands on his hips. George was cute when he was being serious. Of all the things he could have said, Mary was not expecting this.

"Excuse me?" she asked, shocked at the sudden change.

"You are not allowed to touch my penis anymore." He motioned towards his package, as if she did not understand what he said the first time.

"Why?" Mary's face was twisted in horror and outrage.

George threw her a side eye. "Because you use my dick to avoid your problems."

"I do not!" she denied, clutching a hand to her chest. The look he gave her left no room for argument. They both knew that she had used sex as a way to delay doing things she didn't want to do. She huffed, "Okay, but I didn't see you complaining when I gave you a blowjob outside of the insurance office." Mary crossed her arms, back hitting the bed with a bounce. "And I did renew the paperwork, eventually."

"Only because I physically pushed you in, and my ass literally paid the price for it later." he reminded her, Mary couldn't help but smile at the memory. It was the first time she had used a flogger, and it was a prized member of her spank bank. Mary shook her head, no time for reminiscing now- she had to fight for the life of her pussy.

"You can't do that." That penis belonged to her. Mary thought that was well established by this point.

"I most certainly can." he insisted, crossing his arms in front of him. He was right, it was his choice to surrender his body to her. Mary would always respect that. He took several steps forward and leaned towards her on the bed, bracing his weight on his arms. His face pressed close to hers, his breath tingling her lips. "What are you gonna do? Tie me down and forcibly take it from me?" he joked, but his eyes heated with real interest.

Mary groaned and flipped back onto the bed, putting necessary space between them. "Don't make this harder than it needs to be." she grumbled.

"This is for your own good." he laughed, pulling back and continuing to dress. "It's my job to take care of you, and some lessons are harder than others."

"You realize this will be harder for you than me, right?" she gazed at his package, missing him already. He would be so cold and alone without her. He stepped into the walk in closet, likely in search of socks. George could never re-wear the same pair of socks.

"With great power comes great responsibili-ty." he quoted, voice dampened by the fabric surrounding him.

Mary rolled her eyes and smiled.

Nerd.

George re-emerged wearing sweatpants, t-shirt and a fresh pair of white socks.

"Can we talk about the piano now?"

George sighed and climbed onto the bed next to her. "I tried to play again the day after the recital," he started, pulling her into his arms. She snuggled into the crook of his arm, enjoying the feel of the soft cotton on her cheek. "But I just couldn't. Every time I sat on the piano bench I just kept remembering how small I felt and how I don't want to feel like that again." he explained, eyes sad. Mary planted a quick kiss on his pectoral, hoping to soothe any hurt with her affection. If there's one thing Mary could do for George, it was to drown him with love and understanding.

"We're not so different, you know." she murmured, clasping her hand with his. "I felt small when your parents were talking about how accomplished you were." she admitted. She traced the lines of his hand, hoping the contact would give her the bravery she needed. "It's too bad I can't just get off the piano bench," Mary chuckled, hoping some humour would cut the tension that surrounded them. George suddenly grabbed the side of her face and brought it towards his, his eyes a passionate stormy blue.

"Let me help you." he said, closing the gap

between them with a deep kiss. Mary was confused. She thought they were talking about his piano anxiety.

"What?" she asked, either the kiss had triggered a delirium or she was missing something.

"If you can't get off the piano bench, neither should I." George said with a brilliant smile on his face.

Mary blinked. Were they still talking about his parents?

"Until you feel comfortable about your worth," he swallowed hard, "I will play my piano."

"So you want to feel small...together?" she asked, trying to wrap her head around his offer. Would it help her suffering if he was suffering too?

They both knew the answer to that, considering she took immense physical pleasure from his suffering everyday.

"Precisely." he confirmed, planting another deep kiss on her lips.

5

Consequences

*M*istress stumbled around the castle, grabbing provisions for her newly feline Prince. He looked haggard from his journey, and if she wanted to return him back to normal she had to at least keep him alive. She placed two bowls in front of the creature, one filled with kibble and one filled with water. The cat sniffed the pellets and gagged unceremoniously.

Mistress rolled her eyes.

"At least drink some water, male cats are prone to bladder problems." she said, attempting to convince the animal to let go of his human reservations. The feline blue eyes looked panicked for a moment. He leaned down and sniffed the water tentatively.

The Prince let out a long tortured meowl. This plain water was not to his royal standards. The water he usually drank was infused with lavender and had lemon slices bobbing in it.

"Jesus Christ, fine." Mistress grumbled and plucked a rose from her bedside vase, throwing it into the bowl of water in exasperation. The roses were one of the gifts that the Prince frequent-

ly gave her in an attempt to woo her. She told him repeatedly that gifts did nothing to increase her fondness for him. Truthfully, it reminded her how different they were, and how impossible their love would be. She never said that part to him, it would make her seem too fragile. Her role was to take care of him, protect him from things he can't handle.

"Better?" she asked.

The Prince leaned down and took a tentative sniff followed by several experimental licks. His drinking was sloppy, he was clearly unfamiliar with how to use his new cat tongue. She felt sympathy for the Prince at that moment, he really did not know how to live in the skin he was cursed with. Is this how he felt being born a Prince? So many expectations he was supposed to not only accept, but be happy with?

Now that she was certain he was not going to expire immediately, Mistress began to ponder their predicament. She sat at the vanity and combed her hair, the repetitive motion aiding her thinking.

Obviously the Prince had sought out magical help to avoid his marriage. Her heart melted that he would go to such lengths to stay with her. She was suddenly grateful he wasn't turned into a frog. She didn't care much for slimy things. The only source of potential magic that Mistress knew of was the woman who lived down by the bog. Mistress had seen desperate mothers carry their ill children through the water for healing. The children all survived, so she must not be an evil woman. Mistress could not imag-

ine her Prince trudging through filth for any reason, he must have been desperate. Her heart panged that he hadn't told her of his plan. Did he not trust her? Did she note prove herself useful enough for his plights? She always held him and talked him through trade negotiations gone awry or political scandals. Why did he not trust her with this problem? He didn't have experience with nature or being alone at all. He always had staff around him to attend to his every need or discomfort. Had he done this to prove himself? She glanced back at him, now understanding his unkempt appearance.

What a sweet stupid Prince.

She walked over to him, picking him up and carrying him back to the vanity. She carefully combed out the burrs and grass from his fur, *giggling when he started to purr.*

The Prince always did enjoy his hair being played with.

"Did you have fun on your nature walk?" she asked, pulling on a particularly sticky burr. His purring continued, increasing in volume as he rolled on to his back.

"I don't blame you, you know." she said, running the comb through the mud caked fur of his belly. "What's the point of having a kingdom if no one lets you see it?" She finished combing the dark fur and placed the comb back down on the vanity. The Prince didn't move an inch, eyes closed with his belly up towards the sky.

Poor kitty was asleep.

Her heart squeezed for him, it had been a long

journey.

Mistress decided to go see the Witch herself, looking forward to a walk through the marsh to clear her head.

Mary put the pen down on the surface of her work desk. She was the one being a coward, avoiding thinking about the challenge George had given her. He was very clear in his instruction, she had to believe she was worthy as just herself. What did worthy people do? Mary thought about her Mistress, she was worthy of the respect of royalty. She was confident and unapologetic in her actions. Perhaps she could infuse confidence into her work day? That way he would see that she didn't need this silly catholic school type of motivation for self-growth. The image of George dressed as a priest flooded her mind, causing warmth to pool in her panties. She could find a good use for sacramental oils.

Mary shook her head to clear it of depraved thoughts.

The difficulty was that her role as his assistant was subservient in nature. There must be a way to show confidence while still remaining professional.

She gazed at the email signature that taunted her. 'Executive Assistant' implied she was only here to assist George, which was too compliant. Assistants followed behind their superiors, got on their knees for them. Sucked them off underneath the desk while they were in meetings. Did George have meetings? She would have to find out and suck him off during one.

Mary squeezed her eyes shut and groaned.

This was not helping her predicament at all.

She could not think about being his assistant. She needed to be confident and useful at the same time. If she changed her job title he would see it when she sent emails. That would undoubtably show him that she was fixed and his dick would return.

Probably.

Mary was really shooting in the dark here. Did anyone actually shoot guns in the dark? What an irresponsible thing to do. She couldn't imagine George shooting a gun even in daylight. She'd have to ask him later.

Mary changed her job title to 'Head of Communications' and smiled in satisfaction. Since there were no other employees Mary felt comfortable taking creative liberties with her job description. Sleeping with the boss had its benefits. She imagined herself wearing a suit, sitting at a desk in a private office. She would be the one having meetings and being serviced from beneath a glossy lacquered table. Power throbbed and pooled in her core from the thought of it.

"Baby, can you come in here for a sec?"

George called from his office.

"No!" Mary called back, caught up in a whirlwind of defiance. "Oh, yes, sorry, of course." She remembered herself and quickly scurried to the door.

He was climbing down from a step ladder, eyes trained on a black glossy picture frame. Inside was a photo of the couple, wearing matching goofy faces. The picture had been taken at a photobooth at the last company Christmas party. Since they were the only two employees, it consisted of them getting drunk at a chain restaurant in the mall and taking a picture in the photo booth kiosk near the lottery ticket stand. Mary's chest warmed at the memory, mischief igniting with it. She did have power here, regardless of her love's celibacy.

"Can you tell me if this is straight?" he asked, "I didn't think to bring a level." His eyes were still trained on the frame, allowing Mary to slink in and pull her skirt up unnoticed.

"Nope." Mary replied, plunking her ass on his desk. She slowly began unbuttoning her blouse, kicking off the pink high heels she was wearing. George looked over at the sound of the shoes hitting the drab carpet, breath catching when he realized what she was doing.

"Oh, Jesus Christ." he breathed, gulping loudly.

Mary pulled her panties to the side and began to gently caress her folds. She moaned at the pleasure of her hands, relishing in the hungry gaze of her love. His pants were tented already, always so attuned to her.

"Sweetheart," he chastised, face beginning to flush as he watched her. He was frozen beside the ladder, just a man and an erection he refused to let her touch. Fine, he could stand there and watch but she was going to come.

She began rubbing at her clit in earnest, driving towards orgasm. His attention intensified her pleasure, his gaze almost as potent as his touch.

George let out a small groan as she went over the edge, feeling her pleasure despite being several feet away.

"Oh, fuck. I love you." she moaned, shutters racking her body. Suddenly he was holding her as she came down, planting a soft kiss on her softly panting lips.

"Thank you," he said, "you are exquisite." He nuzzled into her neck. A small frustration ignited in Mary's chest. This was not supposed to be a gift for him. He was supposed to be overcome with lust and toss his silly abstinence plot out the office window.

Mary padded his chest softly. "Anytime, handsome."

George quickly buttoned her up again and she returned to her desk. Instead of opening another email, Mary rested her flushed cheek on the cold wood composite surface and sighed.

Being contrary was harder than she anticipated. She felt no more certain that she deserved the approval of George's family, and now she was experiencing dick withdrawals. Had she misunderstood something? Mary thought back to her Mistress, who she regarded as the height of power. She was going through struggles as well, unsure why her Prince chose to struggle without her. Was Mary acting like the Prince about this? Did she assume his parents wouldn't like her without collecting any hard evidence? Mary knew this was a real possibility, she was prone to assuming things. She would not be able to go any further until she knew what her parents really thought of her.

Mary picked up the desk phone.

"George, we need to go see your parents

again."

6

Mistress meets Witch

*T*he swamp was beautiful this time of year. Rays of sun cascaded between the long thin trunks of the trees. Tadpoles swam between Mistress' toes, reminding her that the complicated problems of humans were inconsequential to every other living creature. The fish were only *worried about swimming.*

And not being eaten.

Mistress was suddenly acutely concerned about the possibility of alligators hiding somewhere in the murky waters. She cast aside those fears when she remembered her reason for the trip. If the fumbling cat Prince survived this marsh, she should have no problems.

The cottage was in surprisingly good condition, the wood appearing intact. Whoever lived here must take good care of it.

Mistress knocked on the door gently, surprised by the occupant that answered it. The woman was small with delicate features. She resembled a mouse, the majority of her face pointing upwards in the center. She appeared to be in the middle years of her life, but deep creases in her skin hinted that they were not easy ones.

"Hello." she said quietly.

"Hi," Mistress began, itching to get straight to the point. "Did you turn a very handsome, dramatic blonde man into a cat?"

The small woman's eyebrows lifted for a moment but her brown eyes quickly filled with understanding. Judging by the bluntness this had to be the Prince's woman. She expected her arrival at some point.

"Come in," she opened the door and motioned Mistress in.

The inside of the cabin was rustic and cozy, a large assortment of plants adorned every corner. Her host waved towards the wooden table and

Mistress sat on a surprisingly comfortable stool.

"I did get a visit from the Prince." the woman confirmed, filling two cups with herbs and hot water. Mistress looked at it with suspicion. "It's chamomile, I promise." the Witch smiled, eyes soft. She was quite beautiful when she smiled. Mistress took a tentative sip. The familiar taste of the tea was bold and completely delicious.

"He was very distraught, conflicted between the duty of his birth right and his desire for love." the Witch explained, running her finger around the rim of her mug. "For you, I suppose."

Mistress' gut clenched with guilt at the distress of her Prince. He was alone in a swamp with a stranger begging for help because of her. "Love like that is very rare, I can't think of many royals that would give everything up for a girl they *love." A small smile was plastered on her face, but her brown eyes were haunted.*

Mistress put down the mug, "I don't understand how this is supposed to help him."

"Is he not free from his royal responsibilities?" the Witch explained, her eyes returned to their sharp intelligent shine. "Is he not free to live out the rest of his days next to the woman he was so desperate to love?" she asked rhetorically. Both women knew that was exactly the situation now. The Prince was released of his responsibilities on the account that he was no longer human at all. Mistress recalled his haggard appearance and discomfort doing basic functions such as drinking water. No, this was not the life he deserved.

"Is there a way to reverse his current...predicament?" Mistress asked, careful not to offend the

woman now sitting across from her. She did not think the woman was evil by any means but it's best not to anger anyone that could transform you into an animal.

The Witch pressed her lips into a thin line, pondering her next words carefully.

"There is, but do you want to?" she replied. "Does he want to?"

Mistress' eyebrows raised in surprise. What kind of a question was that?

Of course she wanted the Prince to return. His place was in the castle, where she could take care of him. He belonged on a throne where he had to marry a woman he didn't love and pine after a woman he couldn't have. His place was to be miserable forever. Mistress' heart clenched.

No, neither of them wanted that. But would it be any better for him to stay as a cat? Would he be happy to spend his time catching mice and sleeping in the sun? Okay, so maybe that did sound like something he would enjoy. Would Mistress be okay with never holding her Prince again? Never feeling his warm human body on hers? Mistress closed her eyes to steady herself. This was not about her wishes. The Prince was meant to be a Prince, and she was meant to make sure he stayed that way.

The Witch placed her delicate palm on top of the visiting woman's trembling hand, eyes shining with something close to pity. "The Prince will return, precisely when you are both ready." she promised, eyes soft and reassuring. "When the scales are leveled all will be right again."

Mistress thanked the woman for the tea and conversation, but clearly there was no more that could be done here.

"Can I give you some advice?" the Witch said as she walked Mistress to the door. "Sometimes, it's okay to be selfish."

Mistress gulped, she might as well have told her to take a long walk off a short pier. The click of the cabin door was haunting with its finality. Mistress was on her own now, it was her duty to protect her Prince even from himself.

7

Mary Meets Laundry Machine

George's parents were away on a yoga retreat for a week, so they made plans for a barbeque visit when they returned. That meant Mary could potentially be dickless for several days which was a national emergency. While she appreciated that

George wanted her to be the best version of herself, it didn't mean she was going to take it easy on him.

Mary was really hoping that this plan worked, or else she may truly be stuck in here. George had asked her to switch the laundry while he went out to pick up the groceries. An opportunist, Mary saw a chance to seduce the celibacy out of her man. She stripped down to just her lace panties and shoved her top half into the front load dryer. It was a tight squeeze, Mary's waist was not particularly slender. Hopefully, he would be overcome with lust at the sight of her behind and she would be reunited with his penis at last.

Her heart hammered when she heard his

voice and footsteps.

"Baby, I'm back. Do you need a hand?" His voice echoed in the hall outside the laundry room. "Thanks for- Oh," His voice cut off—he must have seen her.

His steps were now slower, she felt the heat of his legs directly behind her. The anticipation added to her arousal, if he didn't hurry she would start dripping onto the floor.

"What are you doing?" he asked, voice breathy.

"Laundry," she answered, her voice just as unsteady. A warm hand trailed across her backside, leaving a trail of heat and pleasure in its wake. He pulled her panties to the side, exposing her damp folds.

"This particular article looks very dirty," he murmured, rolling the center of the lace in his palms. The motion caused his knuckles to rub against her sensitive heat. A moan escaped before she could stifle it. She had been deprived of his touch for several days, and felt close to the edge just from the minimal contact.

"You know, I think these are hand wash only." he teased, pulling the elastic away from her body. "I better attend to it personally."

He laid down between her legs, so she was effectively straddling his face.

"Oh, god." she whimpered, quickly realizing this plan would not work out in her favour.

His tongue made contact with her clit, still

covered by the red lace. An explosion of pleasure radiated from her center, amplified by the restraint of the dryer. She could not run from his mouth if she wanted to. Her mewls of pleasure bounced around the metal barrel of the appliances, increasing in volume and frequency in tandem with his tongue. When he sucked her clit she was a goner, shaking and spasming on his face. He gently worked her down from her high, raising himself off the floor only when her trembling had stopped completely.

He tenderly removed her damp lacy underwear and replaced it with a clean cotton pair from the bin next to him. The kind gesture warmed her heart.

She loved this sweet thoughtful man.

"I thought you weren't going to touch me." she mentioned, confused but not complaining.

"I never said that," he said, walking away from her.

Mary assumed from the noise, since she was still in the dryer.

"Shall we go eat some lunch?" he offered. Mary attempted to dislodge herself from the appliance, but quickly realized she was indeed stuck. Great, she was going to run out of air and die in an attempt to get laid. Worse ways to go, Mary supposed. Her great uncle died from amoebic dysentery in Mexico, which was a much less sexy way to die. At least now she was wearing clean panties. Her grandmother can rest easy in her grave now that Mary's corpse would not have dirty underwear, thanks to George. Mary smiled, her grandmother would have loved George.

"Would love to, baby." she chuckled, attempting to stay calm. "But, uh, it appears I'm stuck."

George laughed. He laughed hard. "I guess I can call the fire department," he said, followed by the sound of his footsteps. "Maybe they'll use the Jaws of Life?" he continued, referring to the large sheers that are used to cut people out of car crashes. Mary felt like a motor vehicle accident at that moment- a horrific and irresponsible spectacle. Dread flooded her, horrified at the prospect of firefighters having to cut her out of a laundry machine.

"Don't worry, Baby," he reassured her, "I'm stronger than I look."

Luckily her panic had blossomed a fine layer of sweat all along her compressed skin, providing lubrication for his endeavor.

He grabbed her waist with large steady hands and gave one strong yank.

Mary felt a rush of air against her torso as the machine released her. The momentum pushed them back, Mary landing on his lap. Her heart sang in relief - she would live to see another day. She took several deep breaths, grateful for every gulp of precious oxygen. His arms wrapped around her, holding her as she calmed.

The absurdity of the situation suddenly dawned on Mary, and she burst into hysterical laughter. He joined her, unable to help himself. They laughed together until tears rolled down Mary's face and her abdomen was sore.

Eventually their giggles died down, George gently stroking her hair.

"If you're that horny you can just ask for help," he mumbled into her temple. "You don't have to put yourself in danger to get my attention."

Mary rolled her eyes. Apparently when it comes to her, laundry machines are considered weapons. Her incompetence truly knows no bounds. But she would not let him get away with this victory. She knew for a fact she could not just ask and receive his dick.

"Really?" she asked, turning in his arms to face him. The vinyl flooring felt cold against her bare knees. "So if I asked you to pull it out right now, you would?" she questioned, lips unbearably close to his.

"Nope." he said, stood up and walked back to the kitchen.

George was an exquisite and profoundly perplexing creature. Mary dressed and wandered over to the couch in the living room, opening her notebook.

8

Mistress Makes a Plan

*M*istress was pacing around her bedroom, the cat Prince lounging on her
bed.

"The Witch said that the scales were tipped, and
that once they are level all will be right again."
Mistress said, looking at her cat companion. He

was intensely licking and gnawing at something on his belly. She chose to believe he was listening passively.

"So how have you tipped the scales?" she asked rhetorically. "By disappearing you stranded your fiance at the altar, and left your family to deal with the fallout." she explained, her pacing increasing in speed. The Prince stopped his gnawing for a moment, processing her words. He quickly returned to his grooming, clearly unconcerned with the consequences of his actions. She was burning every available braincell searching for a way to undo his curse and we was more concerned about licking his balls. Mistress huffed and stomped over to him, picking the black creature from the scruff of his neck, immobilizing him.

"Pay attention," she hissed. "What do you think will happen if we don't fix this?" she demanded, tossing him back down on the bed. He stared back at her, blue eyes vacant with shock.

"If you think I'm going to clean your litter box for the rest of your life, you are sadly mistaken." she said, "You get a month, tops. Then, you're in the barn with the rest of them." Mistress was exaggerating, but clearly the Prince needed some tough love to motivate him.

That got his attention, he repositioned his feline body to lay facing her, paws crossed in rapt attention.

"Thank you," She curtsied.

"So, in order to undo the damage you caused we'll have to find another husband for your fiance, and another heir to take over." she stated.

The Prince did not look convinced. Mistress ignored his doubt, it did not help the situation,

"This could hypothetically be the same person, but doesn't have to be." Mistress winced when she thought about the Prince's siblings. He had a younger brother that was nice enough and pleasant on the eyes. He would make a respectable husband, if presented properly. The crown was a more complicated matter. The only competent sibling the Prince had was an older sister. She was intelligent and fierce, well educated and beautiful. Mistress remembered the scandal that erupted when the King placed her on the Council instead of marrying her off. Mistress got the feeling that the King favoured his daughter, picking her happiness over tradition. If she played her cards right, he may forsake tradition completely and agree to name her his

heir.

There was a knock on the door.

"Excuse me, Miss," a male voice said, " you're needed in the kitchen."

Mistress perked up at the interruption, ready to take action.

"Of course, one moment!" she called back. The cat Prince lay face up on the bed, belly exposed to the sky. Mistress swooped him into her arms and balanced him on her shoulder.

"Come on, Prince." she laughed, "Time to meet your people."

The kitchen was bustling when they arrived, the cat Prince sticking close to his Mistress. Likely he was worried about being trampled.

"This is it," A plump woman wept into her apron, "this is the year we starve." Mistress wrapped her arms around the sobbing woman.

"No one is going to starve," she reassured, rubbing the woman's back. "What's happened?"

The older woman hiccupped. "I went down to the Granary to pick up the flour and there was none!" She burst into a fresh round of tears. "She gave me the last bag but said that the Sawflies have come again."

Mistress held the woman and bit her lip, deep in thought. The Sawflies were a problem last year, but the infestation was contained to the northern fields which were a smaller portion of the wheat supply. "Don't worry, I'll take care of it." she reassured, giving the large weeping woman a final squeeze.

Mistress scurried out of the kitchens and towards the stables. The cat Prince ran behind her, staying surprisingly quiet. He was out of his element here, had he ever even visited the kitchen or stables?

Mary rejoiced when she saw the caravan parked outside the wooden structure. The trader was just offloading the most recent shipment, his clothes rumpled from the journey.

"Hello, love." He gave Mistress a gap toothed smile, "How can I help you?"

"Any wheat on that fine carriage of yours?" she asked, smiling when she felt her cat companion rub up against her legs. He wasn't used to not having her full attention. This day would be a rude awakening for him.

The scruffy man looked up and thought about

her question. "Don't think so- wasn't on the list." He shrugged.

"Put it on the list," she said, and ran off back towards the castle. Her pace was fast as she hustled to the diplomatic wing. She walked into the office of the trade commander without knocking. The elderly man looked up at her with an unmoving serious expression, but not one hint of surprise on his sagging face.

"New addition to the list for the Eastern Township- flour." Mistress announced. The man did not say a word or twitch a muscle, but looked down and scribbled on his paper. Mistress took that as approval, and continued on her journey.

She solved several more urgent problems before finally collapsing on her bed, exhausted but accomplished. The cat Prince hopped up onto the bed and settled himself on his companion's chest. She lovingly rubbed his head, smiling when he began to purr. Is this the life that he wanted? To be her furry shadow down on the castle floor? She didn't understand how anyone would prefer to be a common cat instead of royalty.

"It's definitely more hectic, outside your ivory tower." she said to her purring Prince. The vibrations penetrated into her chest, lulling the tension away. Mistress hoped that maybe his purring could heal her broken heart as well.

9
George Meets Piano

Mary's phone rang, interrupting her scribbling. George peeked his head out from the kitchen. He had a surprised and perplexed look on his face. Mary very rarely got phone calls, and even more rarely did she actually answer them. She looked at the call display and took a deep breath.

"Hey, Mom." she answered, tone bright. "How's it going?"

"Mary, I need a favor." The older woman's voice was raspy from a life of cigarette smoke. At least she didn't pretend to care about small talk, that saved some time. Mary stood, walking around while she chatted on the phone.

"What is it?" Mary asked. She was keenly aware that George had abandoned his task and was listening to their conversation with great interest, his slender frame leaned against the door frame casually.

"Gerry left the propane on overnight again and I can't afford to get a new one until next month." Gerry was her mother's boyfriend. Mary had no real problems with the man. He was beer bellied and incompetent, a gift compared to some of the previous men in her life. As Mary's father often said, the man 'pickled what few brain cells god gave him'. Still, he was mostly harmless save for the occasional wasted propane tank.

Mary sighed, shuffling around the plans she had for her day. She and George were supposed to go to a board game cafe where she would whoop his ass metaphorically before going home and whooping his ass physically. Mary suddenly remembered that she would not be touching his dick in any way tonight due to his ridiculous abstinence pledge. The man was a virgin for 38 years, you'd think he would be more hesitant to go back to celibacy. I guess instead they could read a self-help book or meditate. Mary actually wasn't sure what people did to improve themselves. So far Mary just didn't think about her problems or cried about them.

In the back of her mind she knew that she should prioritize her own plans, but the habitual thoughts were impossibly strong. It was her job to take care of her mother, she needed more propane for her barbeque grill. Her mother's need was more important than Mary's fun and sexy plans.

"Okay, I'll grab one and drop it off tomorrow." she promised.

"Oh, I knew you'd come through." The older woman's voice was elated. Mary's veins hummed with satisfaction from the praise. Mary would always come through.

She was scared to look over at George, knowing that he would be disappointed. She wasn't wrong. His eyes were sad and definitely a little disappointed.

"Shut up," Mary groaned and flopped down on the couch. George chuckled and walked over, sitting next to her.

"I didn't say anything." he pointed out, lifting his palms in surrender.

"You didn't have to." she admitted, sighing and laying her head on his lap. He stroked her hair gently while they sat in silence. The feeling was so nice, Mary closed her eyes to fully embrace the ecstasy of it. Mary knew she should talk about the conversation she had with her mother, she knew it was important. His fingers felt so good in her hair, she wanted to enjoy the pleasurable tingle of it for a few moments more.

"It's dishonest," she whispered finally, her body relaxed from his motions on her scalp. "That's the problem." That was what George had told her when they first met, when she downplayed her feelings as her boss hired her. Placing other people's needs before her own is dishonest, it made her untrustworthy. When George's parents asked her about herself, the honest thing would be to tell them the truth even if it revealed Mary's less desirable characteristics. Mary tried hard to be many things, honest was one of them. George deserved an honest woman.

George hummed, encouraging her to keep talking.

Mary opened her eyes, not surprised to see her love looking down at her.

Mary reached up and rested a palm against one high cheekbone. George was a very avid reader, unfortunately that gave him the ability to look into and understand her soul. Damn him and his pretty blue pleading eyes.

"You're going to make me talk to my mother, aren't you?" she sighed, resigned to the unpleasant task.

George bit his bottom lip and nodded meekly. Despite all these lessons he was trying to teach her, he really was a shy man. It made Mary smile.

"Okay," she agreed. "On the condition that you play me a song." She lifted up, pressing a passionate kiss on his meek lips. She poured every drop of love she had into that kiss.

Mary put away the rest of the groceries while George located and set up his piano. He did have one after all, she heard his grunts as he pulled it out of the linen closet. She went to investigate when the grunting stopped but no music began. George was standing be-hind the small electric piano, staring at it as if it were a bag of live snakes. Mary stood next to him, joining in the stare.

"Hm." she said with a serious tone. "It doesn't look dangerous to me, but I'm no piano expert."

George swallowed, "The dryer didn't look

dangerous to you either." He turned his head to look at her. His eyes were apprehensive but not panicked.

Mary giggled softly, "Would you like me to get naked and bend over the bench?" she offered, hoping to loosen him up.

George let out a deep breath, "Maybe later." He took a step towards the instrument. "Better get it over with." He paused and looked back at his love. "Will you sit with me?" he asked, holding out his hand.

Mary smiled, heart melting. "Nowhere else I'd rather be, handsome."

George was a very good piano player. Mary wasn't surprised because George was pretty much good at everything except talking. He was even getting better at talking, soon he would be unstoppable. She leaned her head on his shoulder as he played. The song was quiet and introspective, gentle and haunting without being sad. It was a short piece and before she was ready, his hands stilled and the last notes floated away. She was so caught up in the beautiful music she didn't realize her love had the remnants of tears on his cheeks. She began to panic for a moment before she noticed there was a smile on his face. He turned his face towards hers and the love in his eyes was almost blinding. He leaned down and placed a gentle kiss on her lips.

"Thank you," he whispered against her mouth.

"What was that?" she asked, "It was beautiful."

"Schumann's Träumerei, it's a part of Kinderszenen Op.15. It's about childhood, I think." he explained.

Mary returned her head to his shoulder. "Play it again for me?" she requested. She wasn't ready for this intimate moment to be over.

"If it pleases you," he replied, making her smile.

George played the entire variation this time. His fingers pressed harder this time, growing in confidence. Mary couldn't help but imagine her love as a young boy, expressing himself through music when he wasn't able to use his voice. Her heart throbbed in pain to think that just when he was about to enter the world of adulthood, even that outlet was taken from him. No wonder he was wasting away when she met him. When he finally finished, they sat there holding each other.

"Did I mention you're very good?" she murmured against his chest.

He laughed. "Thank you."

"It deserves a proper piano," she commented, using one hand to rub the plastic surface of his current instrument. "Not that there's anything wrong with her."

George winced. "You're not wrong." He placed a peck on her temple. "But it's all we have space for." Mary liked the apartment they lived in, one that used to belong to just George. It was nicer than anything she had lived in before, so she never considered moving anywhere else with him.

"Why not buy a house?" she asked. "If it's money I can try and get an actual job, and I'm sure your parents could-"

George grabbed her face, cradling it in his hands. "I can afford a house," he interrupted her, eyes filled with love and joy. "I just never had a need for more space." he explained, punctuating his sentence with a kiss.

"Oh, you'll think about it, then?"

George didn't answer, he laid Mary back on the bench and trailed his mouth down her neck.

"Right now, in this moment," he murmured against her skin. "I would give you both of my kidneys." His mouth continued on its path down her body.

What a ridiculous thing for someone to say.

"But you would die if-" Mary gasped as his mouth found her center. "Is it later?"

"It is most definitely later." George answered, eyes drunk with love and desire.

George made love to her on that piano bench, momentary forgetting any ultimatum.

10

The Fool

*T*he Prince's youngest brother was a brute
of a man, with broad shoulders and a
thick neck. Mistress watched him as he tossed
hay bales into a nearby carriage. His biceps
bulged with the effort, an impressive display of
physical strength. Mistress could not hide the
disgust from creeping onto her face. His blonde

hair was a dirty mop on his head, he was likely too busy licking rocks to attend to it.

"That's a nice collar for a barn cat." the Fool gestured at the cat Prince, who was currently purring in Mistress' lap as she pet him. The feline immediately puffed up at the words of his brother, an indignant look in his eyes. Mistress rolled her eyes.

"If he was a barn cat at least he'd be useful." she joked. He gave her finger a light bite in retaliation. She jumped and shrieked at the pain, tossing him onto the hay bale.

"Ouch," she held out her finger to inspect the damage. Sure enough a large droplet of blood trailed down her finger. The Prince's brother put down the tool and jogged over to Mistress, grabbing her injured hand.

"Come here, I got something." The young man pulled a rag out of his pocket and wrapped her hand. His fingers were large and calloused, but his touch was gentle. He would make a nice enough husband.

"That's nice." she praised him, impressed at the competence of the bandage. He was clearly not completely useless. "Why aren't you married?" she asked, testing the grip of her hand. He was more or less good looking and came from royal blood, surely he could have his pick of wives?

He let go like she was on fire.

"Sorry lady, I'm not interested." He walked back to his work, picking up the pitchfork. The cat Prince was back in her lap before she could blink, licking her hand in apology. She pet him lovingly, bite already forgiven.

Mistress laughed at the idea of marrying the foolish young prince. "Trust me, neither am I." Her heart was already stolen by a different stupid prince who was currently purring in her lap. "Is there someone you are interested in?" she asked, hopeful that the answer was no.

He froze for a moment, hay falling off the prongs of his tool.

"Doesn't matter." the young man dismissed, resuming the transfer of hay into the carriage.

"Oh, come on." Mistress chided, "I could help you, I have a way of getting things done." she said, putting on her best persuasive tone. The future of the Prince rested on this effort.

"Remember when you begged and pleaded for spiced goat cheese?" she reminded him with a cheeky smile. "Who do you think found the

arthritic old Italian lady that knew how to make it?"

Both princes looked at her with surprise, clearly this was not common knowledge. There was much she did not get acknowledged for, but that was not worth thinking about now.

The large man continued to shovel but trained his gaze downwards, as if the answer to her question rested between the blades of hay.

"The princess." he admitted, face remaining neutral.

Mistress' eyebrow raised.

"Your brother's fiancé?" she clarified.

He grunted, "Yeah,"

This was too perfect. A genetic nightmare for

their children, but that was not her concern.

Mistress hauled the cat Prince onto her shoulder and ran off towards the castle.

The Foreign Princess was loud and daft and con-sisted of 94% bosom. Clearly the younger prince had a very specific preference. Well two specif-ic preferences that wobbled dramatically as she wept.

"Excuse me, your majesty," Mistress slowly opened the bedroom door, setting the prince down next to her.

"Leave me, I'm in mourning." the young woman said, rolling to stuff her face into the silk pillow. Her gown was ornate and colorful, it reminded Mistress of some of the Prince's silk vests. Her heart throbbed at the memory, but she quickly repressed it. There was work to do.

"Mourning what, exactly?" Mistress enquired, she knew for a fact that the Prince had barely spoken a few words to this woman before.

"The loss of my future husband!" she sobbed, kicking her feet violently like a misbehaving toddler.

"Of course, pardon my ignorance," Mistress said, walking into the room and sitting on the bed next to the wailing woman. "Which is exactly why I'm here."

The young woman peered at Mistress through

one bloodshot eye.

"Around these parts when we experience difficult emotions we use visualizations to, uh-" Mistress started, pausing to fabricate a believable story, *"manifest the future of happiness."* she finished, hoping that she was convincing enough. The woman nodded and flipped over, ready for further instruction. Mistress was delighted but kept her face calm.

"Alright, close your eyes," she said, pleased when the woman obeyed. *"Now, imagine what would ease your misery,"*

The woman took a deep breath, "A large and decadent cake," the voluptuous woman whispered, a smile unfurling on her face. Not the ideal answer but it was a start.

"And who is feeding you that cake?" Mistress

asked, picking up the prince from his spot next to her.

"A handsome young lad." the younger woman said, face tinged slightly pink.

"Ah, yes, and what does his hair look like," Mistress walked around the room, focusing on leading the foreign princess to the right conclusion.

"Hmm, fair like gold," the young woman said, "and his cock is large." The young woman's smile was brilliant now. Mistresses stumbled, nearly falling over with surprise.

"Y-Yes, well, what-what else does the rest of him look like?" she sputtered out, steadfast on succeeding in her task.

"Large," the foreign princess said emphatically, practically roaring the word, "big enough to toss

me over his shoulder."

Bingo.

"Yes, he is." Mistress agreed, "Your lost fiancé could never do such a thing with his feeble body,"

The feline Prince made a sound very similar to a warning growl. Mistress rolled her eyes- it wasn't a lie. He leapt out of her arms and onto the bed.

The young woman gasped and sat up in her bed, looking at Mistress with worry. "If he is not the man of my happiness then what am I to do?"

The Prince preened and creeped towards the dramatic woman, signaling that he was going to help as well.

"Oh! What a sweet kitten," the woman giggled

as the cat Prince licked her cheek.

The Prince may not know how to be a cat, but he knew how to flirt.

"A sweet royal kitten," Mistress explained, "the young prince has been looking for him, and I don't have time to deliver-" she continued, her tone melting into one of request. "I know you're in mourning, and I could never insist-"

"Of course, I will!" The foreign princess whisked the now shocked Prince into her arms, and bounced towards the door. The movement of her chest was so wild, Mistress was concerned the cat Prince would sustain a cleavage-related crush injury.

"He's in the goat barn!" Mistress yelled after them, praying for her Prince's safe return.

11

The Prince Flies

Mary watched her prince as he worked.

They planned to visit her mother in the morning, so George decided to do his work now so as not to fall behind. It was a smart and responsible choice.

Too bad Mary was bored and horny, which

was going to become his problem.

He was sitting at the dining room table, typing on his laptop. His shoulders were hunched.

Mary walked over and stood behind him, leaning down to whisper in his ear. Her notebook and pen still clutched in her hand. She set them down next to his computer.

"Arms behind you," she ordered, delighting at the shutter that racked his body. He was still hers.

He obeyed, sitting up straight at the sound of her voice. Mary lifted the blue silk tie up and over his neck, binding his hands together with it. The tie was one of the wardrobe additions that Mary insisted on.

Slowly, she moved his laptop to the other end of the dining room table. Mary was
going to get her revenge today. Her love
watched her closely as she moved, eyes curious but cautious. He didn't know what she
was planning, but he did not object. She
removed her shorts and panties, causing a
flash of heat to pass through her pet's eyes. It
matched the growing heat and anticipation
growing inside of her own core. One of her
favorite pastimes was driving him crazy. She
kicked away the cotton shorts that pooled
on the floor. Mary balled up the panties and
George opened his mouth without having to
be told.

Satisfaction warmed her chest.

"Good boy," she praised, languishing in his

obedience. He groaned softly, voice now muffled by the satin in his mouth. He picked out this particular set of undergarments himself, Mary hoped his reaction would be especially potent. She was quite damp herself, which aided her mission.

She hopped on to the dining room table, parting her thighs to give him a clear view of her intimate parts.

"You used to watch me in the library." she said, it was not a question. He nodded, breaths were already laboured.

"Too scared to move, to touch me." she continued, stroking his thigh with her foot. He moaned and nodded his head again. Saliva was beginning to run down his face, causing a mirroring moisture between

Mary's thighs. His gaze trailed down to her pussy, like a heat seeking missile. What she wouldn't do to touch his missile.

She leaned back, grabbing the notebook and pen.

"You're going to watch me, like you did then. Unable to touch." she commanded, crossing and uncrossing her legs. The moisture now extended to her inner thighs. If she wasn't careful she would lose control. Taking a deep breath, Mary began writing.

Mistress stepped over rotting logs and broken branches.

She wasn't usually a mushroom picker, but the elderly couple who was usually responsible was indisposed with fever. She was very confident on which mushrooms not to pick, but less confident on which ones actually tasted good. Her Prince followed behind her as usual, sniffing every fungus they found. She was pretty certain he had no clue which ones were poisonous, but she found no harm in letting him sniff anyway.

The forest was dark despite it being the middle of the day, the dense foliage obscuring the early spring sun. Mistress quickly filled her pail with a wide assortment of mushrooms, she turned to head back to the trail and was stopped by a large black wall of fur.

Mistress froze, heart hammering.

The bear growled and bared his teeth, warm breath fanning across her pale face. She was going to die here, alone in the forest. Hopefully the Prince was far away, his superior senses letting him see the bear before she could. He could live out the rest of his cat life peacefully nestled into the foreign princess' large bosom.

Mistress closed her eyes and prepared for the inevitability of death, when a loud and aggressive hiss filled her ears.

A small black ball of fur and claws flew past her and towards the bear's head, causing the beast to back away and run off with a wounded groan. Mistress stayed frozen for several moments, not quite believing what had happened. Did the Prince just attack a bear?

Did he just save her life?

A strangled groan drew Mary away from her writing. The energy in the room was stifling with lust. She looked down the table to see her George, flushed and dripping with saliva. His breathing was shuttering and eyes distant. Intense heat flooded her core.

Perfect.

Mary sat up. She put the notebook down next to her, placing both feet on his knees. He jumped at the sudden contact, partially emerging from his trance. His eyes were feral, just a sliver of blue iris.

He had never looked more beautiful.

She leaned forward, holding a hand out in front of his ravaged face. He spit out the ball of fabric into her palm. She tossed it across the room to join her shorts. She walked her feet up his body, resting them on his shoulders.

"Did you enjoy watching?" she asked.

"Yes, sweetheart." he answered, swallowing audibly.

"Why?"

"You are so beautiful, so wet."

"Did you enjoy being restrained?"

"No,"

"Why not?"

"I wanted to touch you."

"Hmm, it's difficult not being allowed to touch, isn't it?"

"Yes, sweetheart."

"Is that all you wanted?" She ran a foot down to his crotch, "to touch?"

"No, sweetheart." he replied, "I wanted to taste."

"Why?" She hooked one foot on the back of his neck and pulled him down to her center.

"You smell so good, and I need to make you feel good."

"Do you want to taste now?"

"Desperately," he whispered, breath kissing

her folds.

"Beg,"

"Please, my love." he whimpered, "Please let me taste you." His eyes flicked up to hers, his hunger now feral. "I need to make you come."

She pushed his head further, burying his face into her pussy. He took action immediately, licking and sucking ravenously.

"When I come, so do you." she instructed. He moaned against her, signaling his agreement. She wrapped her legs around his head, restraining him against her. It wasn't long before she was falling off the edge, his need was kindling to her pleasure.

"Do it," she moaned out, not needing to

specify. He took her clit into his mouth and bit down gently, yelling out with her when she screamed. She milked his tongue, spasming around him violently. She was only vaguely aware that he stiffened against her, signaling that he had obeyed. As the spasms eased, her legs loosened from around him. Her body was spent, but her pet needed his after care. She willed herself to rise off the table and untie her love.

She softly positioned herself on his lap, straddling his now damp pants. She giggled quietly and tucked his face into her neck, running her fingers through his hair.

It was almost half an hour before he opened his eyes again, a drunk smile on his face.

"You flew high, pet." she commented, placing a kiss on his forehead.

"You're a good pilot." he hummed and burrowed into her chest. George was usually very goofy when he returned from subspace. It filled her chest with satisfaction that she could affect him like that.

She carefully slid off his lap and placed the laptop back in front of him. "Get back to work, boss." she ordered, placing another kiss on his forehead. "We've got a big day tomorrow."

"Yes, sweetheart." he gave her a salute before returning to his typing.

Mary returned to her spot on the couch, notebook in hand once again.

12
Princess Found

*T*he cat Prince stuck by Mistress' side as they walked through the royal chambers. He seemed on edge, almost uncomfortable.

Had he gotten used to being her cat companion?

He greeted the townspeople with happy meows every morning and presented himself for petting. It made Mistress smile.

She knocked on the large ornate door, not surprised with how quickly it opened. The King tended to be on the anxious side.

"Oh, it's you." he said, clearly disappointed. The man looked tired, dark circles underneath pale gray eyes. Mistress knew that he loved his children, despite how distant he had to be for his role.

"Good morning, your majesty." she curtsied, stepping past the door when he opened it. The King was still in his period of mourning, and Mistress suspected he had spent the entirety of said period in his room. He was in bed clothes, not a stitch of silk or embroidery on his crumpled frame. He sat at the desk near the window of the large bedroom, leaning forward with his face cradled in his hands. As far as Kings went, he *was relatively young and handsome. Her Prince actually looked remarkably like his father, sans beard.*

Well, usually.

Right now he looked like a cat.

"What do they need now?" the King asked, voice muffled by his palms.

The prince chirped, surprised at the advisory relationship his mistress had with his father. He rubbed his body against her leg, signaling he wanted closer. Mistress picked up her furry companion and placed him on her shoulder.

"The people need an heir," she said, petting her Prince absentmindedly. "Uncertainty isn't good for a kingdom."

The King sighed and stood, walking over to gaze

out the window.

"So you want me to shift from tradition and name my daughter as my heir?" His tone was even, clearly this was something he had thought about before.

"I mean, I didn't say that but-" she began, surprised at his offer.

"Alright." he agreed, still looking out the window.

"Wait, what?" Mistress was completely dumbstruck by the turn this conversation had taken.

"I'm not an idiot, I'm aware my son's are not fit to rule over a turnip field." He leaned forward, bracing his arms on either side of the window. "Truthfully, I've already been considering it since he, you know." Sorrow filled the older

man's tone- he felt tremendous guilt for the loss of his son.

"He told me over and over how much he wanted to abdicate, how miserable he would be, and now he's gone." The King turned around and gasped when he saw the cat Prince snuggled in Mistress' arms. Tears welled up in the older man's blue eyes. "He even put my mother's necklace on a barn cat. What have I done to deserve such scorn?" The King collapsed into the desk chair and sobbed against the fine wood surface.

Mistress' heart dropped at his words.

"Pardon me, your majesty." Mistress excused herself and shut the door behind her with a soft click. Her heart was now racing.

The Prince had tried to give her his grandmother's necklace?

The former queen's necklace?

She had turned it down assuming it was just another shiny thing he bought in order to impress her. He was never a clueless Prince thinking with his private parts, unaware of future consequences. He wanted the scandal of telling the world that she was his Queen. Mistress shut him down, and worst of all she convinced herself it was what was best for him.

How dare she?

This Prince had saved her life and shown her nothing but loyalty. If she hadn't dismissed the depth of his love, he never would have gone to the Witch in the first place.

She would do better now, she would show him that he could depend on her for everything. She vowed at that moment to do whatever she could to release the Prince from the curse, and to let him choose what he wanted for his future.

The Princess was not hard to find if one knew where to look. Mistress knew she would not be in the usual feminine stomping grounds. She was not one for gardening, or lazing in the piano room. The Princess was right where Mistress thought she would be, in the middle of kicking a man in the ass. The large man lay in the grass panting wildly with a streak of blood falling from his brow.

"Good afternoon, your majesty." Mistress said, releasing the cat Prince to the ground. "I have some good news for you."

The Princess nodded at the fallen man, signaling that he was dismissed. He staggered upright and ran off. Mistress pulled a rag from her pock-

et and handed it to the tall woman, pleased that she accepted the fabric with a nod of thanks. Her pale eyes remained guarded as she wiped the sweat from her brow and adjusted her long blonde ponytail.

"Is the war in the north over?" she asked, clearly centered around politics. The cat Prince gave Mistress a look that implied this was normal for his sister.

"Ah, no," Mistress said, "but your father just told me he will make you his heir." Mistress said, bracing for her reaction.

The Princess blinked.

"Okay," she said, tone flat, "and why should I care?"

The Mistress' mouth gaped, once again taken by

surprise.

"Because you will be the first Queen born into the title since, well, ever." Mistress said, bewildered that she had to explain this.

"I see," The Princess ran the rag across the back of her neck, clearly more interested in cooling off than whatever Mistress was saying. The Prince and his sister were clearly alike in the way they absorbed information. "What if my brother returns?" she asked, sitting on the grass to remove the leather bracers from her legs.

Mistress watched as the cat Prince walked up to his sister and sniffed her hand in greeting. She gave a small smile and an awkward pat on the head. She was clearly not a cat person. With how their conversation was going so far Mistress was not entirely sure she was a people person either. The cat Prince walked away from his sister, clearly disappointed with her petting technique.

Mistress sighed and pulled the feline into her lap. "Unlikely." she murmured, screeching the underside of his furry chin.

The Princess looked at the Mistress with wide eyes. "How could you possibly know that?" she said, "My brother is prone to dramatics, he may reveal himself at any moment."

Mistress was growing tired dancing around the truth, it had been a very long few weeks.

"Because your brother was turned into a cat!" she blurted out, picking up the Prince and holding him up by the armpits. She shook him slightly in emphasis.

"That is my brother?" she glanced skeptically at the black animal, who escaped from Mistress' grip and presented himself to the Princess with a flourish of his tail. "Okay, I see it."

Mistress laughed. She loved her Prince, even when he was a cat.

"The Witch in the swamp turned him into this to teach him some sort of lesson." she explained, reclining back and watching the Prince as he groomed himself. He gagged when a particularly long hair got stuck on his sticky cat tongue. Both women laughed watching him struggle.

"She's got a sense of humor, he hates cats. Had a traumatic experience with a sandbox when we were kids." The Princess shared.

"The reason he came to her is because he didn't want to be King." A sharp meow followed by an

eye roll from Mistress. "Didn't want to be married."

Another meow. Mistress rolled her eyes again.

"Didn't want to be married to anyone but me." she clarified under duress.

"I know what that's like." The Princess' eyes were distant, but she quickly returned to the conversation. "Wait, did you say Witch in the swamp? As in, the marsh past the valley?"

Mistress nodded.

"Is this Witch a small woman? Dark hair with a big behind?"

Mistress nodded again, she never noticed the size of the woman's backside but everything else was accurate.

"We must go now," the Princess said, scrambling up to stand.

Mistress retold the entire story of the Prince's curse on the walk to the Witch's shack. The cat Prince lay on Mistress' neck like a furry feline scarf.

"Do you think people will accept that? A woman in charge?" the Princess asked, a hint of insecurity on her face.

Mistress smirked, remembering the games she and the Prince played.

"You'd be surprised."

"You really didn't have to come." Mary muttered to her boyfriend, sitting in the passenger seat smartly dressed in a gray polo shirt with black board shorts. She clutched the steering wheel as they drove to her mother's home, tension filled every fiber of her muscles.

He put down her notebook, exhaling loudly.

"Of course, I did. How else can I protect you?" he said, tone perplexingly serious.

"Defend me," she repeated, "from my

mom."

"From what little you've told me, I can only imagine she's got talons and fangs." he explained, finally indicating that he was joking.

Mary sighed.

"She's not a bad person, I promise. She's just allergic to making good decisions." Mary said, desperately trying to defend her mother.

"But that shouldn't be your problem." George said, throwing Mary a pointed look. He sighed and shook his head, attempting a different angle. "How would you feel if it was the other way around?"

What if Mrs. Python placed all responsibilities onto George's shoulders his entire child-hood? What if it caused him to shut down the part that made him believe he was intrinsically worth anyone's time?

"I would fight her to the death." Mary stated simply. George placed his hand on her thigh, causing tingles to go straight to her core. He didn't have to say any more. They both knew she wouldn't be able to move on with her life and accept love without dealing with this.

Mary deserved love. Mary was good and kind and needed a family that saw that.

The trailer park was cluttered with refuse, making parking a challenge. Mary found a space between an overturned wheelbarrow and what appeared to be a statue made from old soda cans.

Reuse did come before recycle. The large majority of things sent for recycling end up in landfills anyway, so perhaps there should be more old soda can statues. On second thought, aluminum had a recycling rate of 90%, so this statue was likely for artistic purposes. Mary really had a lot to learn when it comes to art. George's parents were probably art people, maybe she should take a picture of it for discussion later.

Mary did not grow up in this particular trailer park but once you saw one you saw them all. Her mother had a tendency to move frequently, probably why Mary was so keen on knick-knacks and home decoration as an adult. She never had the luxury of possessions.

"You don't happen to have a steering wheel lock, do you?" Her eyes shifted to the gleaming silver Prius.

George rolled his eyes and he grabbed the propane tank from the trunk.

"I've got insurance." he reassured, pushing her onwards.

Of course he did.

George was a smart, respectable man. He grew up in a mansion with smart respectable parents. Did he grow up with that dog? The wrinkle ball could easily be twenty years old. The oldest dog in the world was thirty one. Mary shuddered at the idea that his dog was older than her. Mary was a plain girl that grew up bouncing between a trailer park and a downtown apartment. She had no finesse or decorum.

Mary shook her head. George loved her, awkward edges and all. She came here to assert her self worth and earn back the right to touch his dick.

"Mary Beth, you told me you were bringing a propane tank, not another lawyer." her mother drawled from her place in the foldable lawn chair. There was a lisp to her enunciation, caused by the obvious lack of teeth in her mouth.

"Hmm, no fangs." George commented. Mary coughed to hide a laugh and elbowed him in the gut. Her mother's teeth fell out shortly after Mary was born, it was tragic and made her slightly terrified of childbirth. The choice to not get implants or dentures was entirely her own, and was likely too good of a decision for her to make. Mary didn't actually think that her mother broke out into hives when she did something that improved her life, but it sure seemed like it.

"It's nice to meet you, Mrs..." George trailed off, setting down the propane tank.

"Maureen is fine," the older woman shot him a toothless grin. "Gerry, the tank is here!" she hollered, standing from the plastic chair and shuffling back towards the trailer. Her gait was more of waddled due to degeneration in her spine from decades of janitorial work. Gerry popped out of the trailer, tongs in hand and stained apron on. The apron barely covered his protruding belly, the cartoon woman's body graphic distorted. He grabbed the propane tank and carried it to the small barbeque grill, grunting with the effort.

Mary cleared her throat.

She could do this.

"This is the last time." she announced, waiting for a response. The older woman turned back towards Mary, processing what she had just said.

Would her mother scream?

Would she cry?

Mary preferred screaming over crying. If there was screaming she could simply leave.

"Okay." her mother said, and looked towards the couple. "Do you want to stay for lunch? These burgers have been sitting in the fridge since yesterday waiting for the propane."

"Yes, definitely." George answered, rubbing his stomach in anticipation.

"Wait, what?" Mary was flabbergasted. "That's it?"

Where was the fallout?

Where was the downfall of her parents without her help?

Maureen winced, "I had potato salad too, but we ate it instead of the burgers last night." Her face scrunched in contemplation. "Linda might have some extra corn we can borrow. Gerry, can you run down and ask?"

Gerry capitulated, pausing his clumsy fumbling with the propane line. When the man was gone, George headed towards the apparatus.

"Might as well put myself to use," he mumbled and detached from Mary's side, efficiently disconnecting the old tank and attaching the new one.

Mary had the sudden urge to stick her head inside the grill.

She had done this monstrously difficult task of drawing a boundary with her mother and nobody cared.

The sky was not falling, and nobody was crying.

Actually, Mary might cry.

Maureen scanned her daughter's face, "You're upset." she commented.

"I just told you that I'm not going to be your errand boy and you don't even care."

"Errand boy?" Her mother looked confused and then hurt. "Mary, all you had to say was no."

Mary's breath caught.

All she had to say was no?

Surely, Mary had done that before. Horror and embarrassment flooded her when she came up empty handed. Suddenly, George was there. She was wrapped in long steady arms and led towards the car.

"Give us a minute." He excused them, settling Mary on his lap in the back seat. She straddled him, arms wrapped around his head and face buried in his neck. Hot tears finally escaped and landed on his shoulder.

"I am a fool. Imbecile. An idiot of the highest caliber." she wallowed, tears staining his collared shirt.

"No, you're not." he cooed, rubbing her back gently. "Everyone makes mistakes."

Her sobs intensified.

"Not ones that make them grow up with deep psychological wounds that haunt their future relationships."

George gave her a pointed look. He did not have any friends or even talk to anyone until they met, and he was over a decade older than her.

Mary laughed and wiped her eyes with her forearm. "Okay, point taken." She pressed their mouths together, the kiss deep and soulful.

"You didn't do anything wrong," he murmured into her hair. "You felt like you couldn't depend on the one that was supposed to care for you, and that's not right." he validated her, putting her hair in soothing strokes. Her tears slowly dried, breaths slowly returned to normal.

"Now might be a good time for a gift." George murmured against her hair.

Mary sat up, face scrunching in confusion.

George cleared his throat.

"When we were with my parents you said

you felt like you haven't accomplished any-thing. Well, I have a solution for that." George pulled a folded piece of paper from his pants pocket.

Mary grabbed the paper from his hands and opened it, a weary smile creeping onto her face.

She read the small black letters several times, not fully comprehending the words.

"You want to add me as a co-owner of your business?" Mary breathed, shock stealing her voice.

"Yes. It's my job to make sure you know that you are my equal in every way." His smile was so bright Mary's retinas were in danger of permanent damage.

"George, that is so irresponsible and devastatingly romantic."

He always knew what to say when she needed it.

"What are you going to do when my problems aren't fixed with a cuddle and a cry?" she mused, savoring the feel of his touch.

"We love each other," he shrugged. "We'll figure it out."

13

Princess Meets Witch

*M*istress knocked on the door, now familiar with the feel of the worn door on her knuckles. She would have to come visit for tea when this was all over.

The Witch opened the door wide, expecting a visit from her acquaintance. Her face paled *when her eyes glanced at the Princess.*

"Oh, god." the Witch breathed, stepping to the side and letting the group in. Mistress removed the Prince from her neck, dropping him down and allowing him to leap onto the dining room table. Mistress walked over to the fireplace and grabbed a mug and small bowl. She carefully poured hot water in each receptacle, tossing a flower petal in the bowl. She set both dishes down on the table and turned to face the other women, surprised that they were still standing by the door, frozen.

"A hut in the swamp?" the Princess said, tone sharp. "Are you fucking kidding me?"

"Excuse me?" the Witch said, tone still weak with shock.

"I get you enjoyed your little herbs but to become

a witch in the fucking swamp?" the Princess yelled, stepping closer to the Witch. "You'd go to such lengths to avoid me?"

The comment snapped the small woman out of her shock. The Witch rolled her eyes and crossed her arms. "Oh, get over yourself, blondie." the small woman retorted.

Blondie? The Mistress and her cat traded puzzled expressions.

"Not all of us live in a fucking castle. Real estate isn't exactly cheap around here." the Witch said, eyes still pointed towards the heavens in dismissal. She dropped her gaze to the uneven floorboards. "Not for people like me."

"People like you?" The Princess took another step closer, their noses now almost touching.

"Yes." The Witch swallowed, lifting her chin in brave defiance. "Dirty, worthless, pitiful, common-"

The Princess grabbed the Witch by the back of the head and pressed their faces together, kissing her deeply. The smaller woman moaned and returned the embrace.

Mistress' eyebrows raised and the Prince's little cat tongue popped out in surprise.

They pulled apart, panting.

"Well, clearly you two are, uhm," Mistress interrupted, causing the women to suddenly remember they had an audience, "intimately acquainted."

The Princess crossed the room and sat next to Mistress, adjusting her ponytail. This must be a *nervous habit of hers.*

"Princess, I think we were here for Royal business." Mistress reminded the blonde woman, attempting to refocus both women on the task at hand.

The Princess cleared her throat, lifting her chin in a snobby mannerism. "As the future queen, I order you to remove the curse from my brother." she demanded.

The Witch cackled. "I don't think you can be queen while there is still a prince."

"The Prince is unavailable, considering he is currently a cat." the Princess said, haughty royal tone making Mistress cringe.

The Witch smiled, brown eyes lit up with mischief. "Is he?"

The women turned their heads and inspected the feline. He was regal, well-groomed with a diamond necklace. In all ways other than species he was still the Prince.

The Prince let out a deep, sorrowful meowl. He understood where this was going. He contracted his body, slipping the beautiful necklace off his furry shoulders. He jumped off the table and repositioned himself on the window sill, gazing out onto the horizon of the swamp. He could not be both a prince and a cat, could not be both the master and the servant. Mistress' heart panged for him. She could not watch his legacy lay discarded and pooled on the wooden table. Mistress walked over and cradled the jewelry in her hand. It deserved a worthy home.

If she was going to live without the Prince's hu-

man body for the rest of her life, surely she deserved one selfish action?

Besides, she had gone through great trouble to attempt to cure his curse, she deserved a moment of luxury. Without any more thought she clasped the necklace behind her neck, smiling as she felt the instant connection to her Prince.

"Oof!" A loud bang rang through the small cottage. The women looked over at the window, where a very naked and very human prince sat on the floor.

14

Mary Meets Python Again

George put down the notebook, holding Mary's hand from where they sat at the picnic table. The barbeque at his parent's home was so starkly different from Mary's. There were several different vegetables and not one of the meats on the huge grill was processed. His parents were laughing together, Mrs Python wrapped appropriately around Richard while they grilled.

They looked like a hallmark movie. Mary felt approximately two centimeters tall. She gripped onto George's hand, drawing strength from his touch. Together they could do anything.

Before she could chicken out she stood up, "I lied to you."

The older couple looked over at them, watching with rapt attention.

Mary swallowed hard, "I grew up poor and boring and I didn't want you to think that George could do better." she admitted, eyes squeezed shut. "He can do better, because he deserves a girlfriend that is honest."

she continued, confidence boosted when George squeezed her hand. "I assumed you wouldn't like me because I don't have any notable accomplishments to make me worthy." Mary finished, cracking one eye open when there was no response from her audience.

Mrs. Python looked at her with...pride? Tears were welled up in the older woman's blue eyes.

She walked over to Mary and grabbed her other hand, leading her into the house.

"Let me show you something." Mrs. Python said, stepping into the living room. She pulled out a photo album, and flipped through until she found a picture of a brown headed man with his arms wrapped around a young woman.

"Is that Richard?" Mary asked.

"No, that is Paul." Mrs. Python laughed, "He was a scumbag who ended up burning a cigarette hole into my couch."

Mary joined in the laughter, her previous couch had many cigarette holes, but no smelly tenants.

"I didn't meet Richard for another eighteen months after that picture." the older woman continued.

Mary appreciated the insight into the woman that had intimidated her so much. However, Mary didn't quite understand why George's mother was showing her pictures of her shitty ex-boyfriend.

"Why are you showing me this?" Mary asked.

"Because I was twenty five in this." The older woman said, clearly aware that it was Mary's current age.

Was she implying that George was Mary's terrible future ex-boyfriend? He didn't smoke and it was his couch they spent time on, so the comparison was a bit weak. Mary was just about to defend her love's honor when the older woman started speaking again.

"Listen, until you I thought that the only chance of grandkids we had was a toilet seat accident." Mrs. Python said, no hint of jest on her face. Mary laughed, making a note to look up the incidence of toilet seat pregnancies later.

"Just because it took George thirty eight years to get it together, doesn't mean I expect the same from you now." she said, closing the photo album and gathering Mary's hands in hers. "The only thing I expect from you is that you'll be good to him."

Mary's heart filled with love for George and his family. All Mary had to do was love her man deeply and get pregnant eventually. She couldn't speak to her fertility yet, but she couldn't stop herself from loving George and she had no plans of trying.

"I promise." Mary said, overcome with gratitude. She wrapped her arms around the slim woman and squeezed her just a little too tightly.

15
Happily Ever After

*T*he *Princess and Witch squeaked and turned around, giving the man some privacy.*

"The, uh, frogs need inspecting." the Witch stammered, fleeing towards the back door.

"Yes, I will supervise." the blonde woman agreed, joining the hasty escape.

Mistress laughed and walked over to the shocked Prince. She reached up and removed a curtain, throwing the linen on the shocked man's lap. He stood up on shaky legs, tying the fabric around his waist.

"Welcome back," Mistress said, stepping closer to her shaking love. His blue eyes were wide and skin glistening with sweat. He launched himself at her, smashing their mouths together. His strong arms wrapped around her, crushing her chest to his. Their tongues wrestled and souls reacquainted. They parted with a gasp, panting for air. The Prince crushed her body to his, nuzzling his nose into the crook of her neck.

"Oh, how I missed you." he mumbled against

her skin.

Mistress laughed, "You never really left," she pointed out, skin tingling at his closeness.

"Let me rephrase," he said, gazing up at her. "I missed your touch, kiss, and body." he listed, giving her bottom a firm squeeze. She took a deep breath and detached his grip, fighting the molecules that begged her to hold him. She needed to respect his choices, let him make them without her influence.

"What's wrong?" he asked, face contorting from joy to confusion. He sensed her apprehension, now aware of the small shifts of her body that betrayed when she was conflicted. The weeks he spent pressed close to her body as she ran around saving his kingdom had taught him a lot.

"You're a Prince again." she said, hand subcon-

sciously running against the jewels on her neck. She fiddled when she was nervous- a few hours ago it was his fur she was fidgeting with. Now he was on the outside again.

Now that he was back to being a Prince he was no longer welcome in her world.

His blue eyes filled with hurt. "You don't trust me, do you?" the Prince accused. "You think I'm soft, privileged, and I don't have what it takes to survive without my crown." he explained, tone now angry.

Mistress was silent for a moment, formulating an accurate response.

Did she tell him that she was worried he would choose his life of comfort over her?

Now that he'd experienced some hardship, seen

the labors of her life, would he go back to his comfortable role at the castle?

Mistress was sure the King would give him an advisory position at least, his guilt transformational for their relationship.

Could she go back to loving him in secret? Mistress was not sure she could survive the heartbreak, after being so accustomed to his constant presence over the past few weeks.

"Maybe you're right." he said, voice small and defeated.

He turned and walked out of the shack. Mistress felt his absence the moment he walked through the door. She followed him, unable to stay away from her love.

He was sitting on the front step of the deck, look-

ing out at the still water. The frogs were croak-ing, twilight inviting the lightning bugs to pro-vide spectacle to their song. Mistress sat next to the Prince, warm muggy air sticking to her skin.

"I was so blind." he gazed out towards the water, brows furrowed. Mistress knew then his outburst was not about her at all. "There is so much pain in my castle."

"Listen-" she began.

"They were screaming for help and I couldn't hear them atop my pedestal!" he continued, dis-regarding her attempted interruption. "I was so worried about my pointless politics, I didn't see the earth beneath my kingdom was crum-bling." he mused, talking to himself more than anything else.

"It was you, all along." His tone was suddenly

light and distant. "Tilling the dirt with your bare hands while I whined about dinner parties." His eyes were full of emotion when he looked at his Mistress. "No wonder you don't trust me without my crown, I never deserved it. Or you." he finished, voice small.

Mistress didn't speak right away, still trying to control the hurricane of emotion inside of her.

They were both alone.

Foolishly determined to keep their lover free from the tarnish of their troubles. The Prince saw her as his ruler, a deity he could not please without wealth and status. He believed he was only good as a Prince, and wholly inadequate as a man.

Mistress saw him as royalty, a sensitive man who must be shielded from the discomforts of hard-

ship and her unpleasant conflicts. They sat there together but until that moment they were very much alone. She caressed the necklace around her neck, a flag announcing his love for her. The opulent stones used to feel like a cover, a rich table cloth meant to cover a plain undesirable surface.

Why had this brought him back?

According to the Witch the act of wearing the jewels had balanced the scales. She had not worn them before because she felt that their purpose was to mask her deficits and who she was as a person, really.

Is this what she thought about the Prince?

Was she worried that his splendor would over-power her? He had journeyed to great lengths and proven that he wished to stay by her side, *even after seeing the hectic unsavoury bits. He had saved her life, instead of running away to safety. He had earned the place around her neck. She had no shame wearing the loud, dramatic jewelry because she already wore the loud dramatic Prince in her heart.*

"You did survive without your crown. You ate kibble too." she giggled, attempting to break the wall of ice between them.

He groaned. "Don't remind me."

She turned and straddled him, keenly aware that all that separated them was a curtain. It had been a very long time, the Prince being denied his human body. Despite all they had been through, they were still the Prince and his Mistress. They needed to return to that. She placed her hands over his eyes, hiding behind their fa-

miliar games.

"Tell your Mistress what troubles you." she commanded.

His cock hardened and breath shuttered.

"I don't know how to be a man." he murmured with honesty, laid bare by his Mistress. His breath caught when she ground her center on his erection, in a physical reminder of how much of a man he was.

"You didn't know how to be a cat either, and you figured that out." she joked, removing her hands from his eyes. They quickly adjusted and gazed back at hers, filled with love and apprehension. He had acted with bravery and selflessness, risking his life for her. She grabbed his chin and pulled their lips together, kissing him deeply. Their tongues tangled and souls embraced, re-

joicing in the reunion.

"You've always been a man to me, being a prince was just a horrible side effect." Mistress smiled, tracing the planes of his face lovingly. He leaned forward and placed a kiss on the jewels that now lined her neck.

"Why didn't you let me in?" he asked, hurt in his eyes. "Did I not deserve every corner of your heart, even the tarnished bits?" he demanded, hurt intensifying.

Mistress looked down, shame filling her with his words. He grabbed her face and tilted it upwards, forcing their eyes to meet again.

"I did not deserve it." he reassured her, "I was a coward, I let my insecurity keep us apart."

She grabbed his hands and used them to cover

her eyes, allowing her to be brave. "I was scared too. Scared that if you saw how weak I was, I could not call myself your Mistress." He removed his hands, cradling her face in his hands once more.

"Weakness?" His voice was tender, irises a deep and unending blue. "Being scared is not a sign of weakness, it's a sign of humanity." he reassured, placing a chaste kiss on her lips. "I've seen great knights shit in their armor before a duel. They still win."

She really had won.

"You will always be my Mistress." he murmured, placing her hand on his chest. "Protector of my heart."

"And you will be my Prince," he vowed, mirroring his action with his large palm. "Ruler of my *soul."*

They held hands as they strolled back to the castle. Mistress had fashioned the curtain into a makeshift robe. It floated atop the water as they waded back to whatever future laid ahead.

"It won't be easy, you know." she said.

"Please direct me to any point where this has been easy." he replied, unphased at the squelching of mud between his bare toes. Mistress giggled, gleeful at being able to converse with her Prince once again. She had missed his human voice. She had enjoyed the companionship of the cat Prince, but this man was who she loved.

Barely clothed and covered in sludge, without a penny to his name or social power. He had never been more beautiful or more deserving of worship.

"Besides," he added. "I've had to shit in a box for three weeks, there can be no greater hardship."

They walked through the swamp, still dark and foul. The insects chirped and frogs croaked.

The Prince did not gag, not even once.

Mary looked up from the notebook.

Her chest was filled with a bittersweet accomplishment. It was also sad when the story ended, even if everything did work out in the end. Mary's mind tumbled around with the characters she had created, analyzing why she had picked them to begin with. She filed through memories of that time, when she spent her hours gazing at a mysterious quiet stranger.

He was a prince to her, back then. Distant

and powerful in the reign he had over her body and emotions. She longed to retrieve her power, to have him surrender himself to her willingly. The kinky sex was just a plus, really. Just like the Mistress, Mary realized that he wasn't just a prince. He was a man who was complicated, imperfect, and above all human.

He was a man that loved her, and that was where his power was.

Even bound and gagged, he held her entire soul in the palm of his hand.

Mary shut her notebook for the final time, the sound reverberating through the empty library.

She was surprised when he told her they were going to the Library, considering it was a weekend. Mary had learned not to question George too much, when he made plans it usually ended with her orgasm.

George looked up from his book, eyes hungry and light when they met hers.

Mary stood and walked over to the bathroom stall she had used as a personal masturbation haven for weeks. It remained much the same months later. Luckily, it was more or less clean.

Nothing sexy about urine. Well, some people did have kinks for waterworks but she didn't think she was one of them. She made a mental note to ask George what he thought of it.

Mary left the door unlocked, considering the only other living human in the building was very much invited to join her.

Mary pressed her back to the wall next to the door, the same place she had orgasmed many times before. She had used this sanctuary to imagine the depravity of his submission many times. Those memories fueled her arousal, heating her core.

There was a knock on the door, "Are you okay?" her love asked, mirroring a previous encounter. She knew he had fixated on finding her in a post-orgasmic state.

Why not rewrite history a bit?

"No," she breathed, hands palming her breasts. "I need mouth to mouth, desperately." she purred, voice echoing in the small bathroom. Before she could speak another word, George was on her. He pressed his lithe frame against her heated body, grinding a clothed erection against her center.

"Thank god." he moaned against her mouth, plunging his tongue inside. They kissed deeply, hands wandering over each other's bodies desperately. She untucked the white dress shirt from his pants, gracefully removing the belt and unbuttoning them. They parted for breath, George taking the opportunity to trail kisses down her neck and to her breasts. Mary's core was so tight with need, her orgasm would come quickly. She had to slow this down or it would be over too soon.

"Remember the last time we were here?" she asked, moaning as he bit down on a nipple and pressed his groin against her clit.

"How could I forget?" he panted, removing

one hand from her chest to trail it underneath her dress.

"Is this what you wanted to do, last time?" she asked. "What you imagined while you waited for me at the table?"

"No," he grunted. He took a step back and dropped to his knees. "This was." He lifted her dress over his head and dove into her pussy, licking with desperation.

"Oh, Jesus." Mary moaned, shaking when he sucked her clit into his hot mouth. Her plan was backfiring as usual. This man was truly perfect in every way. She gripped his hair with both hands and pulled. He let out a tortured and aroused groan.

"You couldn't have done this," she stuttered, attempting to regain control of the situation. "You were just a virgin."

He rose from between her legs, allowing her to pull his face close to hers. She reached down and gripped his cock, hard and already weeping.

"You were waiting for me to come take what's mine, weren't you?" she demanded, stroking him roughly.

"Yes, sweetheart." he replied, throwing his head with pleasure.

"Give it to me," she commanded, gasping when he lifted one of her thighs and slid inside. Neither of them would last long. This fantasy was too depraved, too close to their hearts.

He thrust into her savagely, restraint run

out. Mary had no willpower left to slow him down. She wanted his pleasure.

"Give me your come." she demanded, joining him when he climaxed.

They stayed there for several minutes, holding each other. His face was nuzzled into her neck, a favourite post-coital nook for his nose. He pressed soft kisses to her neck, causing her to hum in sweet pleasure.

"Marry me." he mumbled against her skin.

"Pardon?" she must have misheard.

"Be my wife." He rephrased, stepping back to look into her eyes. He was completely serious.

Mary blinked. Had she orgasmed so hard she lost consciousness? Was this a post orgasm delirium?

"Are you proposing to me in a library bath-room?" It was a step up from a gas station bathroom, she supposed.

"Right," He realized his mistake, face flush-ing. "Never mind."

Mary rolled her eyes, "Well, you can't take it back now." He looked down, clearly embar-rassed.

"Do you have a ring?" she asked, curious if he had planned this, or it was just an impulse he couldn't restrain.

Mary gasped when he pulled out a velvet box from his pocket. The ring inside was beau-tiful. It was small and delicate, one row of square diamonds.

Simple and genuine, like her man.

"I will," she said, placing a kiss on kiss trembling lips, "but only because you didn't ask."

"How did you manage to rent out the library?" Mary asked, admiring the intricate ring while George locked up.

"A sizable donation to a dog rescue in Guatemala." George winked, shoving the keys into the pocket of his dress pants.

Mary laughed. Of course, her old boss Mr M would have a part to play in every part of her relationship, including her engagement. She'd have to send Esmeralda's sister a gift basket.

They walked the eighty four steps back to the apartment, holding hands and sharing goofy smiles. Mary marinated in the memories that had led them to this moment, to each other really. How the maintenance closure of the library catalyzed their relationship into a romantic one.

Mary stopped suddenly, turning to face George.

"Do you think they ever installed a carbon monoxide detector?"

About the author

S. Nasonov is a romance author with a firm belief that everyone needs to relax. She loves to explore the diversity of power in relationships. All of her character's are kind of weird and that's how she likes them. She lives in a world of neurodivergence, where nice guys finish first and sometimes don't finish at all. She invites readers to crack open a book and put up their feet, they deserve it.

Preview of To Win a Witch

The Princess was hiding again. The young Witch carefully snipped the leaf o the stem, flicking her gaze to the tiny Princess. The young girl was shielding herself in the raspberry bush. Shielding may not be the appropriate word, as her glittering shoes were sticking out between the branches. It was not typical princess behaviour; the Witch was aware of that. Her princess was not a typical one. She was fierce and brave and always spoke her mind, all traits that were frowned upon for princesses.

Discouraged for girls in general, if she was hon-

est with herself. The Witch had never been bold or brash; she preferred to observe and formulate calculated opinions. One had to be observant to be an adequate gardener. Plants couldn't tell you what they needed; you had to pay attention to how they responded to different moisture and light levels.

The Princess responded to pressure by hiding in the raspberry bush.

A finely dressed older woman pushed the glass-paned doors open, round face flushed with anger. It could also be exertion; she was quite a round woman in general. The Witch quickly tossed a shawl on top of the other girl's wiggling feet. Her mother had recently received it in trade for a leprosy tincture. It was made of coarse wool, so it was no tragedy to toss it to the ground. It was likely worth a fraction of only one of the Princess' slippers. The wriggling shoes froze at the stern voice that reverberated o of the glass walls of the greenhouse.

"Princess!" The woman called out, eyes scanning the greenhouse.

"Is there a problem, Ma'am?" the Witch asked, her tone the pinnacle of polite surprise.

The woman cleared her throat, straightened her dress, and smiled politely. The Witch wasn't convinced there wouldn't be retribution if the governess got her sausage fingers on the lobe of the Princess' ear. Last week, she found herself hiding underneath the grand piano to avoid music lessons. The Witch had been delivering chamomile for the King's tea when she heard the screaming from down the hall.

"The Princess is required to attend her lessons; please remind her of this." The woman inclined her head in a curt nod and walked away. The Witch didn't move or speak until the echoing of her footsteps faded away.

"You can't avoid it forever," the brown-haired girl murmured, removing the fabric from the hiding Princess.

"Says whom?" The Princess grunted, extracting herself from the bush. She sat up, pulling a twig out of the long golden curls that framed her face. The Witch rolled her eyes and grabbed a spare piece of twine, methodically removing plant debris from the Princess' hair and tying it in a neat ponytail. The royal girl smiled in gratitude and got to her feet. Although they were similar in age, the Princess towered over her mousy friend,

taking after her father in height. She also inherited his tendency for dramatics, but her bright blue eyes were her mother's—may she rest in peace.

The Witch didn't know much about the Queen, considering she had been bound to her bed for many years before her death. The Witch's mother had always told her not to be grateful for death, but she found it difcult when her majesty's illness was what led the young girl to her closest friend.

The Witch had routinely been the delivery girl for her mother's remedies. She moaned and groaned when asked, but truthfully, she was glad for the chance to explore the castle during her route.

The regular delivery to the Queen's quarters was

a tincture made from ginger, peppermint, and lemon.

"It keeps the food on the inside," her mother had explained.

"What's this one for?" The small girl pointed towards a bottle she had never been to before.

A sad expression the Witch learned later was pity planted on her mother's face.

"That's opium," the older woman explained. She crouched down, voice soft as she spoke to her curious daughter.

"When someone is near death, it makes their passage more comfortable." Her mother looked down at her as if someone had already died.

"Shouldn't we try to cure the Queen?" the Witch asked, unsure why they wouldn't try to make her

better. There was always a way to make someone better.

The older woman closed her eyes and took a deep breath.

Sometimes, when we cannot change the future, we must just make the present bearable," she explained, placing both bottles in the Witch's leather satchel.

The Witch was reminded of those words when she made the final delivery to the Queen. The Chambermaid had grabbed the bottles from the Witch with a whispered gratitude, handing her a single piece of candy wrapped in wax paper. The Witch usually stu⬚ed the sweet in her mouth ravenously, but a small cry made her pause. The delicious treat was just inches from her lips.

A few steps from the Queen's bedchamber door, a mop of blonde hair sat on the floor weeping quietly. The Witch stepped closer; curiosity was her worst trait.

"Are you alright?" the Witch asked, now able to see that the tangle of hair was wearing a very pretty dress. "No." A high voice replied, mu[]ed by snot and expensive fabric. "My mother is dying." The identity of the wailing form revealed itself—a grieving Princess.

"Oh." The Witch said, unsure how to respond. She typically tried to solve the problems that made her cry —she was quite good at that. Death was a problem she hadn't come across, but she knew it was very permanent and impossible to avoid. The Witch felt the weight of the candy in her hand, her only tool at that moment. It

was a remedy of one kind, she supposed. "Well,
would a candy help?" she o☐ered, holding out
the wax paper bundle.

The mop lifted up, revealing large blue eyes. Her
face was splotchy, but the Princess was certainly
beautiful. Her blonde hair was long with per-
fectly maintained curls. She looked like one of
the porcelain dolls the Witch had never been
fortunate enough to have. She would probably
just break them anyway.

The Princess happily accepted the candy, un-
wrapping it and popping it into her mouth.
"Thank you," she said, a small smile warming
her face.

The Witch felt a rush of satisfaction in her chest
at helping the Princess in just a small way. She
couldn't do anything to change the girl's situa-

tion, but she could make her feel better for now.

The Witch had been helping the Princess make the best of her situation every day since then, including shielding her from a cross governess. The girls' eyes met, and they burst into a fit of giggles. The Princess threw her arms around her friend, hugging her tightly.

"Thank you," she breathed, pulling away and brushing the soil o⬚ her dress.

"They're going to catch onto us soon," the Witch said, picking up the basket of herbs and walking over to the bench. "Princesses belong in etiquette classes, not hiding in the foliage." She contorted her voice into the haughty tone of her teacher, earning a laugh from her blonde friend.

The Princess sighed, joining her companion on the bench.

"Don't remind me." Her blue eyes were sad as they carefully bundled di⬚erent leaves together. The Witch didn't like to see her closest friend su⬚ering, even if she benefited from her rebellion.

"It might not be bad to behave a little bit," the smaller girl suggested, her tone careful. She felt responsible for the Princess' welfare—as a commoner, it was her duty to make sure the crown stayed strong.

Her mother had been incredulous when the Witch happily announced the identity of her new friend. She often reminded her to attend to the girl's needs as if they were her own as if they were the needs of the kingdom itself. She didn't need the reminder, honestly. Making the Princess smile caused a flutter in the Witch's *chest, which was motivation enough.*

The Princess sco□ed, tying o□ the twine a lit-tle too sharply. "Easy for you to say," she mur-mured, lips pursed with pessimism. "Have you ever been to a luncheon?"

The Witch laughed and shook her head."The gardeners don't usually get invited." Her par-ents were in charge of the expansive gardens in-side the castle. This allowed them certain privi-leges, such as a greenhouse for growing specific medicinal herbs. Formal events, however, were still well above her family's social class.

"Consider yourself lucky," the Princess groaned, her usual melodic voice tainted with childish anguish. The Witch knew her friend hated royal social engagements; perhaps a di□erent angle was needed.

"What is it that you want to do?" the Witch asked.

"Hide in the flower bush until the earth swallows me whole." Her voice was devastatingly serious.

The Witch laughed. "That was a raspberry plant."

"Oh, you know what I meant." The Princess rolled her eyes and crossed her arms, but the corner of her mouth was raised in a small smile. It made the Witch's palms damp. She was pretty certain she had the most beautiful friend in the whole kingdom.

The Princess sighed and looked up at the Witch. "I want to make the rules, not run away from them."

The smaller girl was surprised by her friend's

honesty. The Witch wouldn't mind if the Princess spent the entirety of her day in the greenhouse with her, but it wasn't about what she wanted. The Princess needed to attend her lessons for the good of the kingdom.

"Do you think they're going to let an unedu-cated, misbehaving girl make any rules?" The Witch proposed, crossing her arms in front of her undeveloped chest.

The Princess pursed her lips for a moment in thought.

"Exactly." The Witch took her silence as agree-ment. "If nothing else, just go to your lessons." She encouraged, placing the last bundle of herbs in the basket. "Besides, who else will teach me Latin?" She shot her friend with a sly look out of the corner of her eye.

The Princess threw her arms around her brown-haired confidant again.

"What would I do without you?" She murmured, face buried into the side of the Witch's neck.

The Witch preferred not to find out.